PITTIE PARTY MURDER

BARKSIDE OF THE MOON MYSTERIES BOOK 8

RENEE GEORGE

BARKSIDE OF THE MOON PRESS

Pittie Party Murder

A Barkside of the Moon Cozy Mystery Book 8

Print: ISBN: 978-1-947177-85-7

For my besties, Robbin, Robyn, Dakota, and Michele
You are my squad!

CHAPTER
ONE

The warble of robins and the whoop of whippoorwills laced the air with the sounds of early summer. The energy of the chirpy melodies put an extra pep in my step.

"I can't believe what a beautiful week we're having." I waved and cooed at my fifteen-month-old gorgeous niece, Journey, and her equally adorable brothers, Jackson and Jericho, who were sitting in a jogger stroller, waiting mostly patiently as their mother, my bestie Nadine Booth, strapped them in. The sleek and wide stroller was specifically built for triplets with seating for three. "Yes, we are," I said in a slightly higher voice meant just for them. They rewarded me with toothy grins, Journey with more teeth up top than her brothers. Their dark cinnamon hair and green eyes mirrored their father's and mine. The Mason genes were strong in them. It made me smile.

"Agreed, Lily. Such a pretty day," Reggie Crawford, our other BFF, said. Reggie was a doctor, the elected town coroner, and a board-certified medical examiner.

"It sure is," Nadine said as she finished securing her babies. She was my uncle Buzz's partner and a deputy sheriff for our county. Buzz had become like an older brother to me since I'd moved to the Bootheel, and Nadine was the sister I'd always wanted.

Reggie was weirdly my mother-in-law now, since marrying Parker's dad, Greer. It had been an intimate ceremony, long overdue, with only a handful of friends and family. It was beautiful, and I cried a lot. In my defense, I was also hormonal due to the baby growing in my belly.

"Ready," Nadine said triumphantly as she unlocked the wheels of the stroller. "Let's do this."

By "this" she meant taking the kids for a walk on the beautiful new walking trail at the city park. Moonrise Parks and Recreation had done a lovely job of paving the two-mile path. It had several rest areas with benches, along with some picnic tables dotted through the grassy center. They even had a brand-new playground. The upgraded bathrooms with running water centrally located in the park were a chef's kiss for this pregnant cougar shifter.

Since it was Saturday, there were a lot of people and dogs on the trail, and I was glad I'd decided to leave Smooshie at home. I'd make it up to my big-headed girl later.

"Ow-wooooo," Jackson squealed. He pointed as a woman walking four proudly prancing corgis on a split leash skirted past us in the opposite direction.

"Yawggies!" Jericho shouted with delight. He kicked his little feet with excitement, and it rocked the stroller on one side.

"Okay, Jer-bear," Nadine chided. "Enough of that."

He laughed loudly in response.

I snickered at my friend. "He's not afraid of you one iota."

Nadine's chestnut hair was pulled back in a loose ponytail, and she wore a hat that had M.S.D., for Moonrise Sheriff's Department, on it. She flashed me an annoyed look. "I can make a perp pee himself when I bark an order, but my cop-tone tickles my kid's funny bone."

Journey's bright green eyes were wide as she

took it all in. Her stoicism in the face of her brothers' jubilation reminded me a little of myself.

"Can I just say how awesome I feel?" I grinned, resisting the urge to pump my fists in the air like Rocky making his historic climb to the top of the Philadelphia Museum of Art's steps. My elation wasn't just because I got to spend time with my wonderful nephews and niece or my two BFFs. Nope. I had a spring in my step that I hadn't felt in a long time. "The last time I had energy like this, I was a freaking teenager. How come nobody tells you that hitting the six-month mark will make the pain and suffering of the first five months so worth it?"

The end of my second trimester was going out with a bang. I'd finally managed to gain some weight. Yay. My shifter metabolism made putting on the pounds difficult, and I was already eating Olympian-in-training calories every day to keep from losing more body mass. Needless to say, the extra pounds thrilled me. I'd made a comment to that effect, and my bestie Nadine had threatened to throat-punch me.

"Those six-month hormones are amazing," Reggie said. Her glossy black hair was pulled back into a messy bun. She wore a lavender razorback tank top with matching leggings. Even her tennis shoes were lavender. The color looked amazing with her dark brown eyes and pale skin.

"Unlike you," Nadine complained. "I was a beached whale from six months on, but even I still look back on the energy I had then with some envy. Those days are over."

Nadine looked far from a beached whale in her gray shorts and a Moonrise S.D. T-shirt. She'd lost all the baby weight and had added extra muscle and tone to her physique over the past year. Even so, looking at the three J's, I could see why she was tired.

"I imagine triplets take it out of you." I looked down at my belly, now the size of a volleyball. "Thank heavens, this is a womb for one." I had on one of Nadine's hand-me-down maternity workout tops. The top was light blue with yellow daisies on it. Super cute but a little roomy on me. I didn't mind one bit, though. I was grateful that Nadine still had maternity clothes to give. She'd originally planned to give them to Goodwill, but after she boxed them up, she'd forgotten they were in her garage. Goodwill's loss was my gain.

"One or three." Nadine flicked her hand in a gesture of dismissal. "It's all exhausting. Enjoy the surge while you got it. That's when all the nesting happens."

I hadn't started nesting yet. Not in the way that most people talked about it. Parker and I had discussed getting the nursery painted, but I kept changing my mind about colors. "I guess I better get to getting on the crib and stuff. I just hate to spend the money. It's all so pricey."

Reggie's knees went high as we picked up the walking pace. "The bigger your belly gets, the tighter your wallet gets," she said. "I remember worrying about every nickel and dime when I was pregnant."

"No lie." Nadine shook her head with a laugh. "Kids are expensive. The diapers and food for these three are like adding a mortgage to our monthly expenses. But don't you even worry about a crib. I have three of them that are about to go into storage."

When I gave her a surprised look, she sighed and said, "Journey's figured out how to crawl over the top of the rail, and she's rallied the troops for a full-on mutiny. I'm convinced that girl is either going to be a rocket scientist or a criminal mastermind."

"Not my Journey." I reached over the top of the stroller and tweaked her cherubic cheek. She gave me a magnificent, open-mouthed smile that showed off her four top teeth. "She's an angel."

Nadine snorted. "Not even. I found her, Jer-bear, and J-man sleeping under her crib this morning with a package of chocolate chip cookies empty next to them. I'd put the darn cookies in a top kitchen cabinet. I have no idea how they got up there to get them. And you know Buzz has great ears." She looked exasperated. "He swears he didn't hear a darn thing. Anyhow, we're investing in toddler beds this week."

The story made me laugh hard. Reggie was right there with me.

"It's not funny, you guys," Nadine whined.

"It kind of is," Reggie said with a snort.

Nadine flipped us off, and we laughed even harder.

"Whatever." She adjusted her shorts. "You guys are mean. Have you been getting any weird cravings? I wanted bean burritos all the time. The farting was horrible."

"I crave everything," I told her. "Lots of spicy food, too. I mean, I like heat, but I've been taking it to some five-alarm extremes lately. At least it hasn't been giving me any heartburn."

Reggie grinned. "I had heartburn my entire pregnancy."

"They say that chronic heartburn when you're pregnant means your baby will be born with a full head of hair," I said. "Is that true?"

"CeCe had a mess of black hair, so it might be true," Reggie mused. "But scientifically, I have no idea why it would work that way."

"Maybe all the acid stimulates hair follicles," Nadine interjected.

I chuckled. "That would only work if your stomach doubled as a uterus."

"What do I know?" Nadine shook her hands out as we continued our pace. "I'm street smart, not book smart."

"I'm not sure that applies to this situation," I said. "You can't street smart medical science."

"People do it all the time," Nadine countered.

"And that turns out so well." Reggie shook her head. "I see those people in my office every week."

"Regardless, I haven't had any heartburn, so I guess my daughter is going to be bald."

"Unless she's a cougar like her mom. Then she'll be born with fur everywhere," Nadine said.

I stopped in my tracks as the horrifying idea of giving birth to a kitten in the hospital settled in.

Nadine and Reggie walked a few more feet before they noticed that I was no longer beside them.

"I was kidding," Nadine told me. "You aren't going to give birth to a fur-kid."

"You don't know that." It had been a worry of mine for several months. "She could be a shifter, and if she is, can I even raise her here in Moonrise?"

"You need to reel it in," Nadine ordered. "And did you say she?"

My slip made me grin. "Yes," I told her. "It's a girl."

"Oh my gosh!" Nadine gushed. "We're having a girl." She leaned forward and said to Journey. "Did you hear? Aunt Lily is having a girl."

Journey looked like she didn't care, but the boys smiled.

"Yep," Reggie confirmed. "And she looks like a normal, healthy six-month fetus without any signs of fur, fangs, or claws."

"I can't believe I am just now finding out about this!" Nadine's excited tone allayed my fears and brought back my earlier elation.

"We just found out yesterday with the ultrasound, and I wanted to tell you in person." I'd been getting monthly ultrasounds from Reggie, who was acting as my obstetrician. Considering my nonhuman status, I couldn't take a chance on a doctor who didn't know-know me. Frankly, I was so grateful to have Reggie. "I planned to tell you today, so here I am telling you. You're going to have a niece."

Nadine's dimples deepened with her grin. "That's the best news, Lils. I'm so happy for you and Parker."

"We start the Beautiful Beginnings birthing course this week." Reggie had recommended the classes for Parker and me. "It's every Wednesday night from the beginning of the sixth month until the end of the ninth. I'm nervous and excited."

"Fantastic," Reggie said. "You're going to like Larissa. She's a good teacher and an even better doula, if you don't mind the occasional scent of patchouli and, uhm, herbs."

I snorted a laugh.

Nadine arched her brow, and Reggie said, "It's legal now."

"True," Nadine said. "But it still feels weird hearing about it."

Two pregnant women—a pert blonde and a tall brunette—walked past us at a fast pace. The brunette wore a shirt that said, 'Closed for Business' with an arrow pointing to her groin.

I snarfed when they were out of earshot. "Hilarious."

"It was funny, damn it," Nadine agreed, but she didn't sound amused. "It seems like everyone is having a baby these days."

I gave her a curious look. "Are you jealous?"

"Yes," she admitted. "I don't want any more kids, but I miss being pregnant."

Before I got pregnant, I would've scoffed at her response. But I coveted every moment my little girl was cooking inside me. Every time she moved, it reminded me that Parker and I had created a whole person with our love. I could see missing this feeling.

"I have a sympathy belly at my office," Reggie offered. "You know, if you want to relive the glory days."

Nadine hooted. "No, thank you. The weight, I don't miss." Her expression pinched. "When they were inside me, I knew they were safe. Protected. Now that the three of them are walking, I'm afraid all the time that they're going to get hurt. It makes me feel helpless."

"That doesn't change no matter how old they

get," Reggie said. "You have to hope for the best because motherhood is the one job where you'll never be prepared for the worst."

I knew what she was saying was true. I had raised my brother Danny, and while he hadn't been my son, I worried constantly that I couldn't protect him. In the end, my fears had proved all too real.

"I'm sorry, Lily," Reggie said. "I didn't think..."

"It's okay," I told her. They didn't know me when Danny was still alive. I'd moved to Moonrise less than a year after his death, but I hadn't told any of them about him for another year or two. Admittedly, the pregnancy had been bringing up all kinds of feelings, though. Stuff that I'd thought I'd dealt with.

I gave Reggie a sympathetic look. "You're absolutely right. There's no preparing for the worst, so it's best not to dwell on all the things that can go wrong. Instead, we can be thankful for all the things that are going right.

Nadine nodded. "Damn straight."

We had made two full laps and were working on a third when I saw Nadine's gaze pivot as we walked past the bathrooms. I followed her gaze.

Near the backside, there were two men standing close to each other and having a quietly heated argument. There were too many people around having way too many conversations for me to focus in on exactly what they were saying, but I caught some of the back and forth. Whatever had started the fight, it had devolved into threats of bodily harm if one of the guys didn't shut his mouth. Or something to that effect, then the taller man, who had on a black stocking cap, shoved the other man, a blond guy in jeans and a collared shirt, against the wall.

"Hey!" Nadine snapped.

At her sharp call, Stocking Hat Dude let the other man go. Without turning around, he took off across the park at a jog. The blond guy against the wall, however, took off toward the community center at the other end of the park.

"Did either of you get a good look at that guy who took off across the way? The one with the hat?"

I shook my head. "He never looked in our direction."

"Maybe it was a woman," Reggie said. When we both gave her an incredulous look, she frowned. "I said maybe."

"I heard a little of their fight. They were both men," I told her.

"Stick to the postmortems, Doc." Nadine clucked her tongue. "Leave the detective work to the pros."

"Like me?" I asked.

Nadine made a sheesh sound. "No, goof. Like me."

"Okay, Columbo." Reggie shook her feet between the next few steps. "This is the last lap for me. My calves are getting sore."

"Lightweight," Nadine teased.

"Six miles is plenty for those of us who don't have to chase down bad guys," Reggie countered.

Nadine snickered. "Fair point."

When we finished the last mile and got back to the community center parking lot, Reggie and I helped Nadine get the three babies into the minivan. "Parker thinks we need a vehicle with more seating," I lamented.

"Because you do," Nadine said.

I grimaced. "I'm only having one small person."

Reggie's dark brows raised. "So did I, and neither of your trucks is going to give you the space you need. Trust me."

I looked at Martha, parked between a green four-door sedan and a white mini-SUV, and frowned. "I don't know if I can get rid of her."

My frown deepened when a silver sports car pulled into the parking lot, and the guy with a blue stocking cap stepped out from between two trucks and got in.

"Was that the same guy that we saw earlier?" Nadine asked.

I nodded. "I think so."

Nadine grabbed a pen from her console and wrote the license number down on her hand. "It's probably nothing," she explained. "But it won't hurt to run a plate."

Afeter work on Wednesday, I was eager to get to the community center for our first class. Unfortunately, Parker was slowing our roll. It was bath day at the shelter, so he'd been late getting home. On top of that, he'd been wet and dirty from head to toe. Normally, I would've joined him in the shower, but time was ticking.

I sipped on my third strawberry protein shake of the day and watched the minute hand on my antique cuckoo clock click forward to the two and called out, "Come on, Parker. It's ten after five. We're going to be late for class."

We had signed up for Blissful Beginnings, a birthing class at the Moonrise Community Parks and Recreation Center, a few weeks earlier. The course focused on relaxation along with natural, drug-free births. Most drugs didn't last very long in my system, so the class sounded like a good alternative.

"We're not going to be late," Parker called out from our second-floor bedroom.

A fluttering in my stomach made me smile. "Your daddy is so slow. He's going to make us look bad in front of all the other parents."

I slugged back the rest of my shake. Early on in my pregnancy, when I had lost a few pounds, it worried Reggie. So, I reached out to my witch BFF Hazel Kinsey, from my hometown in Paradise Falls, the place where I'd grown up, and she'd put Reggie in touch with her bear shifter mother-in-law, Anita Baylor. Anita had assured my friend that weight loss in the first two trimesters was normal for our kind.

I'd had to increase my meals to eight times a day and more than double my calories. Hence, the shakes.

Smooshie, my seventy-five-pound red and white pit bull, rubbed against my calf and whined. I'd noticed lately that the more pregnant I got, the whinier *she* got.

"It's okay, pookie-bear. I'll always love you," I

said sweetly to my furkid, then I shouted up the stairs again, "Parker, come on!"

"We have forty-five minutes," he hollered back. "And it's only a fifteen-minute drive."

"I don't want to be the last to arrive," I groused. Being last meant everyone in the room turned to stare when you entered. I'd spent most of my life blending in and going unnoticed, and that's the way I liked it. "Get your cute butt moving."

Parker strolled into the living room from the hallway. He wore a pair of lightweight charcoal-gray track pants with a black T-shirt that had our new logo: a pit bull line drawing that had a pawprint heart attached to the end. Our name, Moonrise Pit Bull Rescue, was in neat block lettering underneath.

His blue eyes went soft when his gaze met mine, and a broad smile lit up his handsome face. "My cute butt is moving," he said. "Just got to grab my keys." He arched his brow at Smooshie, who was now perched between my legs, her tongue lolling to one side as her tail whipped back and forth against the back of my thighs.

I patted my loveable boop between the ears. "Someone wants to go with us," I told him.

To which he laughed, "She's gonna have to get used to not being the baby anymore."

I squatted down to hug my sweet girl. "You will always be my baby."

She shoved her nose under my armpit and wagged her tail as if I'd just told her we were going on a run.

"Nope. Next full moon," I promised. I hadn't been shifting as much as I used to, and Smooshie missed our miles of running in the woods. It was another thing I'd consulted Anita Baylor about. She'd told me that changing into my animal form wouldn't affect my pregnancy at all and it was fine to shift anytime I wanted. However, having a child with a human was new territory for shifters, so I kept my furry days strictly to the full moon cycle, the only days the urge was stronger than I thought it was safe to fight.

"I still can't believe we're having a girl," I said softly.

He put his hand on my stomach. "I can't wait to meet her."

Smooshie said, "Ah-rah-roo," with an emphasis on "roo."

"You're fine," Parker told her. "You've eaten, you've pooped, you've had a treat, and we won't be gone long. Go hang out with Elvis."

My gorgeous pibble gave him a wide smile, her tail wagging so hard it engaged her whole butt.

"I'm not falling for it," he told her. "Go."

Her ears flattened, and her tail dropped as she trotted over to the front door and flopped down.

I pursed my lips and pouted, "She's soooooo sad."

He chuckled. "She's so spoiled."

"That too," I didn't deny. I gestured at the furry barricade blocking the exit. "What now?"

He arched his brow at me. "If you want to be early, we step over her."

"Fine." I felt mean as I slowly slid the front door open, dragging Smooshie's melodramatically limp body in the process.

Parker snickered.

"Don't laugh," I grumbled as I tried not to giggle. I knew she'd be fine. Smooshie and Elvis could be left alone for several hours without any incidents, but since the beginning of the second trimester, my pupper had been acting particularly needy.

We stepped over her head and closed the door as we exited the house.

I let out a sigh of relief as we walked to Parker's dually pickup. "That was a close one."

Parker put his arm around my shoulder. "Honestly, I thought she was going to the birthing class with us.

My eyebrow quirked up. "Do you think we could bring her?"

He guided me toward the passenger door. "I think they have a no-dogs-allowed policy." He gazed off into the distance. There were some dark clouds on the horizon. "Is it supposed to storm today?"

"Forty percent chance of scattered rain," I said. "Nothing major."

"I've got an umbrella in the back, just in case."

"Good thing," I teased him as I patted his cheek. "Sugar melts."

"Har har." He opened the passenger door for me and gave me a boost into the cab. I could see his eyes narrowed in consternation as he walked around the front to the driver's side.

"What are you thinking about?" I asked him when he climbed in.

He frowned as his gaze met mine. "That it might be time for a new vehicle?"

"Not this again," I said, trying to keep the annoyance out of my tone. "It's nice that you helped me up into the truck, but you know I can still get in and out without any problems."

"I'm talking about the baby. We need something

bigger. I mean, look at all the crap Nadine and Buzz have to pack every time they take the triplets anywhere."

I flashed him a sharp stare. "I think the operative word in that last bit is triplets." My influx of hormones had made me edgier than I liked. I softened my tone. "I'm having one child. How much room can she take up?"

"From what I hear, it's a lot." He started the dually and got on the road. "We need something that has more seating and storage room."

"I am not a mini-van kind of gal," I told him.

"No, but you might be a mini-SUV kind of gal." He leaned over, one hand on the wheel, the other digging in the console between us. "Here." He handed me a bifold brochure-sized folder from Moonrise Motors.

"Huh," I grunted. "I'm sure they have great mini-SUVs but I'm not interested."

Parker reached over and opened the brochure. Inside the fold was a price quote.

I nearly swallowed my tongue from sticker shock.

"That's a whole-four-years-at-a-university kind of money."

Parker shook his head. "Have you priced any

universities lately? It's a good deal. The mini-SUV is used, but it's only a few years old and has less than thirty thousand miles on it. On top of that, it's in beautiful condition. It will last us for years."

I rolled my eyes and clucked at him. "Thirty thousand dollars is more than I want to spend on a vehicle. Your truck has a backseat. We'll make it work." I didn't like owing anyone anything, especially money. "Besides, we can't get rid of your truck. We need it for the rescue."

He stared at the road. "I wasn't planning on trading in my truck."

"I've told you before. Martha is off the table." Martha, my small green pickup, had been with me for a lot of years. She might not be pretty or completely reliable, but I loved her.

Parker snorted a laugh. "As if anyone would give us any money for that hunk-a—"

"Hey!" I cut him off. "No badmouthing the truck that brought me to you. If it hadn't been for Martha breaking down at your dad's garage, we might not have ever met. I certainly wouldn't have met Smooshie." I didn't have to imagine what my life would be like without her or Parker. I'd spent too many years alone and feeling unloved. I never wanted to go back.

"All right," he allowed. "I'll give that to the old girl. But Lily, we need another vehicle. One that's family appropriate."

I fought back the urge to flat-out say no again, and instead, I shot for a compromise. "Okay, but let's look for something more used and under ten grand."

Parker shook his head. "Woman, you are going to nickel and dime us right into the rich house." He chuckled at his terrible joke.

I groaned. "That's the goal." With a new baby on the way, we had a lot of extra expenses, not the least of which would be more hospital bills. I had finally paid off the time I'd gotten run over when I stopped a murderer-kidnapper from escaping with my friend Opal tied up in the trunk of the car. Getting an expensive vehicle was out of the question. It would strangle our already choked finances.

"I can see this is upsetting you." Parker turned off our road onto the one that led into town. "I'll let it go for now," he said. "But I hope you'll keep an open mind, okay?"

I dropped my hand onto his thigh and gave him a grateful squeeze. "I'm open to something used that won't cost a kidney."

He nodded. "Fair enough."

The rest of the short ride into town was in comfortable silence. I stared out the window, trying to quell all the fears racing around in my head as we passed the Rusty Wrench on the way into town. I put my fingertips against the window, remembering how it all started as we passed the four-way stop where Smooshie rescued me from a speeding car and I'd met Parker. It was amazing how much my life had changed in the span of a magical few minutes.

"Dad's working late," Parker mused.

I saw Greer's truck in the small parking lot, and the bay doors were open. There were four other vehicles in slots.

I smiled. "Business is good."

Parker grinned. "Business and life."

I knew the "life" comment was about my doctor bestie. "Reggie feels the same way," I said. "Those two were meant to meet at this time in their lives. The right time."

Parker put his hand on mine. "I know that feeling."

His love eased the anxiety in my chest.

"Lily?" Parker slowed down for the turn into the community center parking lot. "Are you okay? I don't want you to make yourself sick with worry."

"I'm not worried," I lied. "Just a little...restless."

"It's too bad we aren't legally married. I could enroll you as a dependent. That would make the medical bills one less headache."

Parker had medical insurance through his medical retirement from the Army, but those benefits didn't extend to hand-fasted spouses. To the government, I was no better than his live-in girlfriend.

I winced. "You know I would make it legal in a heartbeat," I told him. "But the military will do background checks. I don't have a birth certificate, at least not a government-issued one, and my driver's license is a fake." It was a really good fake that my friend Hazel had acquired for me before I moved to Moonrise. "And I don't want the government looking too closely at my not-so-legal social security number, either."

Parker looked unconvinced. "We'll put a pin in it for now, but I hope you know you can talk to me if you're worried about anything. We're a team, Lily. You can trust me with your worries."

I nodded. "I trust you completely." It was *me* I didn't trust.

CHAPTER
THREE

The classroom was on the second floor, above the aquatic center and next to the fitness area. Since the third month of my pregnancy, my sense of taste, hearing, and smell had all become even more sensitive than what's normal for a shifter. The scent of skunky body odor and deodorant sprays, along with the clanking of weights and the heavy footfalls on the treadmills, made me lean into Parker. He casually put his arm around my shoulder and held me firmly enough to make me feel less anxious.

I gave him a grateful smile. "I hope the room doesn't smell this bad," I whispered.

"Gosh, same," a woman standing behind me said.

I turned to get a look at her. She had short, dark, layered hair that managed to look trendy. She had a few extra pounds that gave her face a roundness that softened her pointy chin and sharp nose. There were fine lines under her gray-blue eyes and on her forehead, and I felt a strange sense of relief that I wasn't the oldest mom in the bunch.

"I'm Tess, by the way." She shook her head and crinkled her nose. "Ewwee. Someone has been generous with the body spray."

A short and stout woman with curly brown hair jumped into our conversation with, "This place smells worse than my oldest daughter's laundry pile. She plays sports year-round for Moonrise High, so you know it's bad."

I remembered how gross my brother Danny's clothes had smelled when he was a teenager, and he hadn't even played sports. I smiled at the shorter woman. "So, this isn't your first child?"

She snorted. "Nope. There are two before this one. Gina, the smelly one, is fifteen, and she is constantly spraying body spray everywhere, and Gabby is ten, so she's just starting to smell." She rubbed her rounded stomach and chuckled. "I'm sure this little guy will eventually smell just as bad."

Tess, the trendy-haired mom-to-be, said, "Oh, you're having a boy. How nice."

A tall, lanky man wearing a light jacket beamed with pleasure as he put his arm around the stout woman. "We are," he said. "I'm Gail Ford."

"And I'm Andi," the stout woman added. Her eyes pivoted to my stomach. "Do you know what you're having?"

"Lily and Parker." I gestured between my guy and me. "We're having a girl." Parker and I had considered waiting until the birth to find out, but when the time came to say yay or nay, I'd wanted to know. "I'm glad we found out. I've had enough surprises in my life."

"I agree wholeheartedly," Tess said. "Getting pregnant at thirty-five was enough of a shocker for me." Her gaze went distant for a moment before snapping back to the present. She tucked her short hair behind her ear.

Because she looked uncomfortable with her confession, I told her conspiratorially, "Our pregnancy was also unexpected."

She snickered and nudged me with her shoulder. "We should form a club."

There were four other couples hovering at the closed door, but I'd seen two more couples huddled together a little farther down the hall. One of the men, a guy with dark blond hair, looked familiar, but I wasn't sure where I'd seen him before. He wore a pale-yellow golfing shirt that fit well through the shoulders and chest but clung to his middle spread.

I grinned to myself. Parker had started to gain a few pounds in the past few months. I was eating more, and so was he. It didn't matter. Even with the extra weight, he was drop-dead sexy.

"What are you thinking about?" Parker murmured in my ear.

"You, of course," I replied.

He made a satisfied hum sound, then said, "We could skip the first night, you know, if you have a hankerin'."

I giggled and gave him a rib-tickle with my elbow. "Tempting, but no."

"Why's the door locked," one of the men asked. "Where's the instructor?"

I looked around, then back to Parker and muttered, "I'm wondering the same thing."

"I'm here!" Larissa Merriweather, whose hair was colored a dark purple, hustled past us. "Sorry, I had car problems on the way over. But I set up the room this morning, so we should be good to get started right away." She took keys from a pouch around her waist and unlocked the door. "Everyone, go on in. Please silence your phones and put your purses and any electronics in the cubbies on the far wall. This is a relaxation zone. No tech allowed."

Parker and I filed into the room right behind Tess. We all headed toward the cubbies. I put my handbag in the opening below Tess'. Parker took his phone off his belt and tucked it into my purse's side pocket.

"I have small kids at home," a sandy-haired woman who had been standing with the dark-blond man said. "What if the babysitter calls?" She looked familiar as well.

"This is a two-hour class," Larissa replied. "We will take a five-minute break at the top of the hour, and you can check your cell phones at that time." She forced her smile wider. "These are the rules so that everyone can get the maximum value from this course. If you feel like they're too difficult to follow, this might not be the class for you."

"It's fine," the sandy-haired woman said, followed by a nervous giggle. "I'm sure the kids will be fine, and our sitter has my mom's number as well."

"Perfect." Larissa nodded, then continued her instructions. "After you put your stuff away, grab a pillow and a ball from the tubs, then pick a spot on one of the yoga mats. There's enough for one set per couple." She glanced back at the weight area. "My assistant should be here shortly to help anyone without a partner." She raised her thumb to her mouth and bit on the nail. Then, as if realizing she was gnawing publicly, she immediately dropped her hand to her side. "I'm so sorry, everyone. This is a terrible way to start our first class."

Tess pointed to two empty mats beside each other nearest to the cubbies. "You guys want to sit over there?"

I brightened at the idea. The fact that Tess wanted to sit next to me made me feel like a popular girl. "Sure."

"Fine by me," Parker added as if he had a choice. "I'll get the pillow and ball." Those items were in tubs lined up on the far wall.

"Grab some for Tess, too," I said.

He arched his brow at me. "Sure."

Tess smirked. "He didn't have to do that."

"He doesn't mind," I assured her. "Where's your partner?" I didn't ask about a husband because I wasn't old-fashioned enough to assume.

"I don't have one," she said. "It's just me and the kid."

"Oh. You don't have a friend who can do this with you?" I asked.

She patted my arm. "It's okay, Lily. I'm capable of doing this on my own."

Even so, my question had been presumptuous and rude. "Of course, you can. I didn't mean to imply you couldn't."

"Don't even give it a second thought," she said genially. "The baby's healthy, and I'm happy. That's all that matters to me."

"Okay, moms and dads." The instructor clapped her hands. "Let's get started. Everyone, have a seat on the floor. Mommies on the mats. Daddies behind them. Use the pillow as a prop to get comfortable if you need it."

Parker took my hand as I got down on the mat with ease. Tess had to bend over and put her hand on the floor to ease her way down.

"My name is Larissa Merriweather. I've been a certified doula for ten years, and I've attended dozens of births and taught four classes a year for the past five years. I've seen it all, so if you have any questions about anything pregnancy or birth-related, I probably have the answer." She laughed as if she'd made a joke. "For some of you, this isn't your first pregnancy, but regardless of your previous experiences, this class is going to help make the rest of your pregnancy and birthing journey as painless and carefree as possible."

There were a few murmurs of hopeful appreciation.

"At Beautiful Beginnings, we focus on readiness," Larissa went on. "We'll spend every class rehearsing various techniques that will prepare our moms for labor and delivery. And dads and partners, I haven't forgotten you. You're crucial to a successful, easy birth. My assistant..." she looked around and grimaced "...wherever the heck he is, will be teaching foot and back massage techniques to our dads and partners, to help our moms with pain relief and comfort during labor. I'd like everyone to practice these techniques daily so that when the time comes, you're all prepared." She gave us all a sly grin. "Homework is a mom's best friend."

The room filled with chuckles from the partners and nods of approval from the moms.

I leaned back and grinned at Parker. "I'll expect you to study twice as hard as everyone else."

He kissed my ear. "We're talking naked massages, right?"

I shook my head and rolled my eyes. "You're so bad."

"You two are adorable," Tess groaned. "I may have to move."

I choked out a laugh. "Sorry."

"No, you're not," she countered with a grin. "And you shouldn't be. It's a perfectly lovely thing to be pregnant and in love. My husband was the same way."

"Your husband?"

"He died a few years ago. I still miss him." She rubbed her stomach. "Some days more than others."

"Wow." Tess was a widow. I could see the pain in her eyes when she said she missed him. It wasn't a lie. Awful, I thought. She was too young to wear that mantle of sadness, but I knew all too well that tragedy didn't care about age. "How old was he?"

"Thirty-two." Her eyes glassed with unshed tears. She dabbed at them with the bottom of her shirt. "Stupid hormones."

"That's young," Parker commented.

"Car accident," she explained, but it didn't quite ring true for my internal lie-o-meter. I got it. There were things in my past that I fudged the details of because the truth was too terrible to talk about. A tear slid along her nose, and she wiped it away with her fingers. "You know what, this is supposed to be a happy time." She forced a smile. "Let's keep it happy."

"You got it," I said.

"There you are," the instructor said as a tall man with dark hair and a healthy physique walked into the classroom.

He was in gym shorts and a tank top, his tan skin glistening with sweat. He wiped his brow with a small towel. "I got on the treadmill and lost track of time." He scanned the room. "It won't happen again." His gaze shifted to Tess before going back to the doula.

"Parents, this is Trevor Peters, my assistant. He's a doula-in-training. For those of you who are unfamiliar with the term, a doula is someone who can help provide physical, emotional, and educational support before, during, and after your pregnancy."

Trevor grinned. "Hey, everyone. Again, sorry I'm late. Really glad to be here."

As he dropped his gear at the cubbies, one of the fathers asked Larissa, "Do you have a medical degree?"

"I have a nursing degree, and Trevor is a lab technician at Two Hills Women's Clinic."

A woman snapped her fingers. "That's where I've seen you." She leaned back against her partner, another woman, and said to her, "I told you he looked familiar."

Trevor gave the two women a toothy smile. "That's right. I've worked with the creation process of making babies for a few years, and now I want to help with delivering the final products."

More giggles ensued.

"Just kidding." Trevor was a little too charming, a character trait that made me distrust him.

Larissa's expression flashed with irritation before she plastered on a fake smile. "However," she continued her previous explanation, "work in the medical field is not required. A doula is certified to act as an advocate for the mother and be there for everything that a doctor can't or won't bring to the table." She waved off the subject. "But that's not what this class is about. I'm going to be teaching you and your partner everything you'll need to have a successful and comfortable birthing process." A sly smile crested her lips. "Well, as comfortable as passing something the size of a large cantaloupe from your vagina."

There were snickers and groans at the comment. I let out a soft grunt of recognition when my gaze fell on the blond couple again, and I realized where I knew them from. I leaned back against Parker and made a subtle gesture in their direction.

"I've seen that guy," I whispered.

He glanced in the direction I indicated. "Who?"

I flicked my gaze to the blond man and back to Parker. "He got into a fight with someone in the park on Saturday. If it hadn't been for Nadine, he'd have gotten his butt kicked," I whispered. I'd told Parker about the incident earlier in the week, so he knew what I was talking about.

It was his turn to grunt. "I know him, too. That's Wells Neeley, the guy who owns Moonrise Motors. I didn't know his wife was pregnant. He didn't mention it when I was there yesterday, but I mostly talked to one of his associates."

"Maybe he sold someone a lemon, and that's why they wanted to punch him," I joked.

I glanced over at Wells and his wife, and I caught him looking back in our direction. He quickly glanced away.

I grimaced. "Oops. I hope he didn't hear me."

"He'll get over it," Tess assured me. "Salesmen have thick skins."

"You know him?"

She scoffed, then shook her head. "No, not really."

My lie-o-meter didn't out-and-out ping, but I got the impression there was something about Wells that rubbed Tess the wrong way. Maybe she knew the wife? It didn't matter.

Maybe it was the fact that Wells was in my birthing class, or maybe it was because I didn't want to buy a car, so I felt the urge to prove the dealer was a dud. Or maybe I was just nosey. Whatever the reason, I decided to make it my mission to find out why Stocking Cap Guy had threatened him to keep his mouth shut in the park.

Larissa explained the methodology behind the class. "The purpose of the Bradley Method is to teach your partners to be your birth coaches. Dr. Robert Bradley believed that pregnant mothers needed six things to have a medication-free, comfortable birthing experience: complete relaxation; deep abdominal breathing; darkness; a quiet, intimate space; physical comfort from a partner; and closed eyes for focus."

She grinned. "You can thank Dr. Bradley for your men getting out of the waiting room and into the birthing chambers. He believed that the presence of a loving husband greatly increased comfort to a laboring wife, and he was right."

She nodded to two women on one yoga mat and

added, "And I extend that belief to the presence of any loving or caring partner. Having someone who cares about you in the labor and delivery room makes a huge difference."

She clapped her hands again. "Let's go around and introduce ourselves to the group, and let us know if this is your first child, starting with you two." She pointed to a young couple to the right of her, a dark-haired beanpole of a man with a hook nose and a dark-haired woman who was waif thin. She also had a larger nose that reminded me a little of Barbara Streisand. Maybe the nose wasn't as prominent, but it was similarly shaped.

"I'm Donna, and this is my husband, Sal," the woman said, taking charge. "We're first-timers."

"But not last-timers," Sal joked.

Donna let out a *hah*! "We'll see how this one goes."

The next couple was Gail and Andi, who we'd met outside the classroom. With his jacket off, I could see Gail had a farmer's tan, giving him pale shoulders, dark arms, and a dividing line across his forehead from where he normally wore a hat. He spoke for them. "I'm Gail, and this is my wife Andi." He rested his hands on her shoulders and gave them a gentle squeeze. She patted his fingers.

"This is our third." He beamed a smile. "It's a boy!"

There were several congratulatory responses from the other parents.

Andi gazed up at him, and I could see the love between them. "We have two beautiful girls at home, Gina and Gabby, but as you can tell, Gail is excited to have a son."

Someone clapped, and a few more of us, including me, joined in.

"Thanks," Andi said. "We're excited."

Next was Wells Neeley and his wife. "I'm Wells," the man said.

"I'm Jeanine," the woman continued. "This is our third and fourth baby." With a gush of excitement, she announced, "We're having twins."

The announcement was followed by some gasps and claps in the room.

"Oh, Lord," Tess groaned. "Can you imagine?"

I leaned toward her. "My best friend gave birth to triplets." Nadine and Buzz loved having triplets, but the thought of squeezing more than one baby out of my hoo-ha sounded about as much fun as... well, squeezing more than one baby out of my hoo-ha. "I can't even imagine. One at a time is plenty."

"Agreed," Tess muttered.

"These will be our last, for sure," Jeanine added. "But we're thrilled."

"Would you share with the group why you chose Beautiful Beginnings for this pregnancy?" Larissa asked.

Jeanine rested her hands on her baby bump for two. "I had my first two naturally, and I want the same experience with these two. My OB wants to deliver the twins early, and she's pushing for a C-section, but I really want to avoid getting cut open if I can help it. I'm hoping the classes will help."

"They will," Larissa assured her. "Over eighty-six percent of all mothers who take these classes have successful natural births."

The next pair were the two women Larissa had addressed earlier.

"I'm Anna, and this is my wife, Lizzie. I had our son last year, and Lizzie is having our daughter, so in a way, it's not our first time, but it's our first time." She wrapped her arms around her wife's chest. "It's weird being on this side of the birth."

Lizzie laughed. "You're telling me."

"It would be nice if *all* the spouses could take turns carrying the babies," the brunette woman from the couple next to them joked.

There were some laughs from the women and groans from the men.

"We're Pete and Jackie Reynolds. First-timers. Probably last-timers," she teased. She had long, dark brown hair and wide hazel eyes. "Hey, if you get it right the first time, no need to do it again."

Pete, who was built like a boxer, shook his head but grinned. "This one snuck in on us, but we're getting used to the idea of being parents."

Jackie rolled her eyes, but she looked pleased.

It was our turn after them. "I'm Lily, and this is my husband, Parker. First-timers."

"Don't you run the pit bull rescue?" Anna asked Parker.

He nodded. "Just outside of town," he replied.

"I adopted my sweet Polly from you guys a few years ago when you were still located in town."

Parker gave her a curious look. "I don't remember you."

"I mostly interacted with a woman named Theresa, but we met. Polly's name was Lita when she was at the shelter."

His eyes brightened. "Oh, Lita. White with a black spot in the shape of a goblet on her back and a super sweet disposition." I loved how Parker didn't always remember people, but he never forgot a dog.

Anna's smile showed her pleasure that he remembered Polly. "She still has a sweet disposition and that cute spot, although I think it looks more like a trophy."

"The sweetest," her wife agreed. "She's already the best big sister to our son."

"We've got two of them at home," I told them. "And I can't wait for this little one to meet them."

Tess shifted uncomfortably when it was her turn. "I'm Tess." Her smile looked nervous as she peered around the room. "I'm a first-timer."

I frowned as my internal lie detector pinged.

"As you can see, I'm doing this one alone." Tess glanced down at her feet and tapped her toes together. "I'm okay with it, though."

"Tess, of course," Larissa said. She gestured to her assistant. "You will not be alone. Trevor will partner with you for the classes, and I will supervise him when you go into labor, and we'll both be there for you when the time comes."

Tess nodded. "Thanks."

Trevor walked over and knelt in front of Tess. I could smell the heavy scent of sweat and body spray as he held out his hand. "It's a pleasure to meet you," he told her. "I'm grateful for the opportunity to go on this miraculous journey with you."

"It'll be a real hoot," Tess replied.

"Maybe not so much cologne, though," I said before I could stop myself. I gave him an embarrassed shrug. "Sorry, I'm having some trouble with smells."

"Oh, Lord, me too," Jackie said.

Larissa's eyes flashed with irritation. "I think it's a good idea for everyone in our group to respect the moms with sensitive noses. Let's agree that we won't wear any heavily scented perfumes, lotions, or deodorants during class time."

Trevor looked only mildly embarrassed as he got up. "It won't happen again," he told her.

Tess chuckled. "No worries," but she looked as relieved as I was that he'd backed away a few feet. "I look forward to, uh, working with you."

Larissa said, "We'll meet every Wednesday evening for the next twelve weeks through your sixth, seventh, eighth and ninth months. By the end, you all will be experts on expecting. Don't be surprised when we start losing classmates in the last two months, because babies are unpredictable and will surprise you when you least expect it." She gesticulated. "A happy bonus, we'll all get to know each other better and, from my experience, a lot of you will become fast friends for years to come."

She went on to explain more of how the class would be structured, and it sounded like Parker was going to have his work cut out for him.

When it was over, Tess leaned in. "Fun, fun," she said. "I look forward to seeing how much trouble we can get into."

"Me too," I told her, feeling better about the whole process. "It's going to be great."

CHAPTER
FOUR

The next Wednesday, our second class was all about back and foot massages, and I can tell you with no uncertainty I was here for all of it.

"Yeah, right there," I encouraged Parker as he worked a particular knot on the pad below my big toe. "You have never looked so sexy."

Parker arched his brow at me but kept rubbing.

Tess moaned softly as doula-to-be Trevor did the same for her. She glanced down at him and grinned. "I apologize for the noises. I can't help it. It feels good."

"I'll take all noises as compliments," he assured her.

"You can do the same," I told Parker.

"Uh-huh," he uttered. I could see a smile peeking at the corners of his lips.

"Okay, parents," Larissa said. "Let's take some deep cleansing breaths on this last minute of the massage, and we'll call today another success."

"Heck, yeah," Lizzie exclaimed. "Complete winner."

"And partners, make sure you're practicing these techniques every day. The massages not only help to relax our moms, but they also help reduce pregnancy pains before, during, and after labor. The better your technique, the easier life will be for our moms."

"You mean I'm going to have to do this after the baby is born?" Pete joked.

Jackie gave him a playful backhand and said, "Only if you want a happy wife."

"Happy wife, happy life," Gail jumped in as he rubbed his wife Andi's feet. "At least that's what my grandfather used to say, and he was married for sixty-eight years."

"Couldn't quite make sixty-nine?" Wells joked.

"Wells!" Jeanine pressed her fingertips against her chest as if scandalized.

A few of the men laughed. Even Parker managed a smile. I rolled my eyes and shook my head.

"Har har." Andi poo-pooed him with a flourish of her hands. "Don't quit your day job, Wells." There was a familiarity to the way she spoke to him. Had they known each other before this class? I hadn't gotten a chance to talk to the car dealer at the first class. He and Jeanine hadn't stuck around to mix and mingle with the other parents. This time, Larissa had brought snacks, and it gave us an opportunity to be social. Yay, Larissa. I'd developed a rapport with Andi, so she might be a source in my quest to get all the nitty gritty details about Wells.

As the class came to a close, most of the parents, including Andi, had congregated by the table of fruit drinks and healthy snacks as soon as Larissa declared that class was over. I beelined for the protein cookies. They were snickerdoodle-flavored and tasted better than "protein cookies" sounded.

Gail and Andi approached Parker. "We've been looking for a new dog. We had a geriatric pit-hound mix that we adopted a couple of years ago. He developed some severe health problems last year, and we had to say goodbye a few months ago."

Andi's eyes went glassy.

Gail put his arm around her. "It's been hard on Andi. She hasn't wanted to get a new dog because the idea of replacing Albert felt like a betrayal. But..."

"I've been so lonely without a furbaby curled up against my legs," Andi finished.

"I can imagine," I said sympathetically.

The fact that they had adopted a geriatric dog made me like the couple even more. Puppies were an easy sell when trying to get our rescues forever homes, but we had a few older dogs that would most likely live their entire lives at our shelter.

"Are you guys looking to adopt now?" I asked. It felt like a complicated undertaking to introduce a new dog into the house with a baby coming, but I knew that with the right people, it could work.

"Not adopt," Gail admitted. "But maybe foster." He nodded at Parker. "Are you looking for fosters? We'd be interested in taking in a dog for a few months. At least until the baby arrives."

"With the option to fail," Andi added.

"We're always looking for foster families." Parker's face was alight with anticipation. Finding good people willing to foster a rescue pit bull wasn't easy, and he was excited at the prospect. "Why don't you come down to the rescue this week or next, and we'll get the paperwork started. There is an application process, but as long as everything goes well, we could have you fostering pretty quickly."

With our dogs, even a few months in a house

with constant attention could make a world of difference to their temperament and their lives.

Of course, Parker would make sure that Gail and Andi's home was suited for fostering, and our rescue would provide food and any medical care the dog would need.

Wells and his wife, Jeanine, joined us. "With two kids, two on the way, along with two high-strung yorkies, I couldn't imagine taking another dog into the mix," Jeanine said, "But I've watched the videos your volunteers post, and I'll admit, I am often tempted to throw caution to the wind."

I beamed a smile at her. "They're super-cute derps."

She grinned back. "I've seen clips of your Snoopy. So cute."

"Smooshie," I corrected automatically, but not in an unfriendly way. "And thank you. She's the sun and the moon."

Parker laughed. "And Lily is the stars." He shook his head hang-dog style. "Meanwhile, Elvis and I are stuck on Earth."

"Keeping Smooshie and me grounded." I tugged his ear, and when he dipped his head, I kissed his cheek.

"You two are too sweet." Jeanine cast a wistful

glance at Wells. "Someone I know could take lessons."

"Dude," Wells told Parker. "You're making us all look bad."

Sal rubbed his finger down the top of his hook nose. "Speak for yourself. I treat Donna like a queen."

"Damn right." Donna grinned. "But address me as 'your majesty,'"

The banter was fun and light, and I decided I liked having pregnant friends. It gave me visions of a future where all our children grew up together and became lifelong friends. Maybe Larissa had been right in the first class about the bonds we would make.

Pete jumped in and said teasingly, "It doesn't take much to make Wells look bad."

"That's rich coming from the guy who had to have his wife beg me for a job."

Jeanine's hand clamped onto Wells' wrist. He looked genuinely shocked that she'd done it. Jeanine gave us all a gritty smile. "Pete is a great mechanic. Wells is lucky to have him working at the dealership." Her knuckles turned white as she gripped him harder. "Isn't that right, honey?"

"Sure," Wells replied, nonplussed.

Pete's wife, Jackie, used the lull of the moment to change the subject. "Lily, you said you were having a girl. Have you picked out any baby names?"

I brightened at the question. "Not yet, but we're bouncing around a few ideas."

Parker put his arms around me from behind and rested his hands on my belly. "Grunhilda Euphemia," he teased, knowing full well I wasn't going to allow our daughter to be named after a mythological evil witch whose name had been evoked to scare children. My child would not be named for the shifter boogeyman.

Wells must've picked up on the look on my face, because he literally guffawed before saying, "I guess Parker's not making us look bad anymore."

His comment made me itchy. "I won't be giving my kid any name that might cause her to get her butt whooped behind the bathroom at the park."

The blond butthead blanched. I was petty enough to put a mental tick in the 'Lily wins' column.

Izzie, who had been getting fruit punch, looked up and commented, "That was oddly specific."

When I flashed my eyes at her, she looked unnerved.

She took a step forward. "Wow, in this light, your eyes look glowy."

Crap. In my irritation, my cougar had slipped to the surface. Not enough to freak anyone out, but enough for someone to notice something different. I blinked, and I shoved my beast way down.

Parker's hand slipped into mine, grounding me back in reality. A reality I loved and cherished. I glanced up at him and gave him enough smile to say I was okay.

Tess was packing up her bag near the cubbies on the far wall where we had stored our purses and such. I headed toward her to say goodbye.

When I got close, I saw her pull her hand out of one cubby and quickly take a handbag from another.

"Do you need any help?" I asked her.

Startled, she dropped a phone I hadn't seen her holding when she slid the purse strap over her shoulder. "Oh, hey, Lily."

I stooped down and picked it up. The screen had a countdown for trying the password again. "Here." I tried to give it back to her, but she waved it away.

"That's not mine," she said with a shrug.

She wasn't lying about it not being hers, but it had fallen from her hands, and the countdown screen hadn't started on its own. "You sure?"

Tess shook her head. "I just found it near my bag. Someone must've accidentally set it down in the wrong box." That pinged my lie-o-meter big time. When she saw me looking at the countdown, she shrugged. "I was trying to figure out who it belonged to."

Another lie, but since she wasn't spilling her secrets to me, it meant she really wanted to keep them.

"That's Wells' phone," Jeanine declared with surprise as she came up behind us. "Why do you have it?"

"Oh." I held it out to her. "I found it on the ground. It must've fallen out of a cubby." I regurgitated the nonsense Tess had tried to feed me. There wasn't any sense in stirring up drama over it.

Tess cast me a brief but relieved glance.

"That man," Jeanine chided. "I swear he'd lose his head if it wasn't attached. He's been so scattered lately. You'd think he was the one pregnant." She shook her head. "Good thing I love him."

Tess gave a terse nod, then forced a smile. "Good thing."

I handed the phone to Wells' wife. "Work trouble?" I ventured. "Or something else?"

Jeanine looked sullen. "Nothing like that." Her eyes

shifted across the room to her husband. He'd moved off to a corner with Pete, and it looked like they were in a heated argument. I reached out with my cougar senses to try and hear what they were saying, but all I caught was Pete saying, "I won't do it," and a not-so-nice version of "screw you" to Wells before Jeanine put her hand on my forearm and drew my attention back.

"Thanks," she said. "It's so great to be surrounded by women going through the same experience."

"I agree." I'd been thinking the same thing earlier. "And all our kids will grow up together. How awesome is that?"

Tess simply nodded.

Jeanine confided, "I didn't do this with my last two, and honestly, it was kind of lonely. I practically had to drag Wells kicking and screaming to this class, but I just reminded him that I'd be popping two bowling balls out of my vagina." She smirked. "He fell in line pretty quickly after that."

I laughed. "I bet he did." I wondered if trying that one on Parker would work to deter him from trying to add another vehicle to our property tax and insurance bill.

Tess rubbed her empty left ring finger. "My

husband had bent over backward, trying to make everything easy for me when I was pregnant."

My brow furrowed. Tess had said this pregnancy was her first. I'd felt the lie. Was this the reason why? Had she not only lost her husband but also a child? A pit widened in my stomach.

"Was?" Jeanine asked.

"He died," Tess told her.

"I'm so sorry. How long ago?" She gave Tess' belly a meaningful glance.

Tess gave a derisive snort. "Long before this one took up residence."

It was a half-truth.

"Oh." Jeanine's expression was contrite. "I shouldn't have assumed. Is the father..."

"Not in the picture," Tess replied. "He was a five-vodka-shots decision." She laughed. "It was an anti-Valentine's party. He was cute, and it had been a while. Not one of my brighter moments. But, hey, I don't regret this little one, not one bit. She's a happy accident."

Everything about her confession sent my lie-o-meter into the red. What was she hiding? I wanted to know almost as much as I wanted to find out about Wells Neeley and his assailant.

"Does he know?" Jeanine asked. "The father, I mean?"

Tess arched a brow. "He doesn't."

"Why not?" Jeanine pushed.

Jackie, who was getting her bag from a cubby, jumped into the conversation with, "Because it's nobody's business, Jeanine."

Jeanine blushed. "I didn't mean—"

"No worries," Tess assured her. "It was a one-and-done. I haven't seen him again since that night."

Another lie. I tried to keep the consternation out of my expression.

Jeanine lifted her hand in a wave. "I better go. Wells is standing by the door."

"Don't keep him waiting," Jackie urged her. Her voice held a hint of ridicule.

The crestfallen look on Jeanine's face as she hurried off made me feel sorry for her.

"You didn't have to do that," Tess said. "She didn't bother me."

"I call bull on that one." Jackie picked the cuticle around her left thumbnail. "Jeanine is always a bother."

"Have you known Jeanine long?"

"Her whole life," Jackie said. "She's my cousin."

I narrowed my gaze. "You don't like her?"

"She's always had a princess complex. My aunt couldn't have any more kids after Jeanine was born, so they doted on her hand and foot."

"Is that such a bad thing?" I asked.

"They turned her into someone who can't take care of herself. It's the reason she ended up with a guy like Wells." Jackie waved her hand as if to dismiss the conversation. "I'm sorry. I don't know why I'm saying all this. Jeanine isn't a bad person. She just drives me nuts sometimes."

The way she'd said "a guy like Wells" was another confirmation that my initial reaction to the man wasn't out of left field. Still, she looked flustered, which meant my mojo was working overtime. I had to be more careful when I asked questions. I didn't want to turn Beautiful Beginnings into a confessional.

"I get it," I told her. "Family can get under your skin like no one else."

"Exactly." Jackie gave me a thankful smile. "And all these hormones coursing through our bodies don't help."

"Amen," Andi said, joining the conversation. "I threatened to ground my fifteen-year-old until she was thirty yesterday because she left half a glass of milk on the counter, and when she got huffy about it, I started crying." She shook her head and laughed. "That took the wind out of her teenage sails."

"Something to look forward to." Jackie grinned and gave us a three-finger salute goodbye.

"Girl Scout," Tess mumbled. "Figures."

"Pardon?"

"The salute," she explained. "They use it in the scouts."

"Huh." I had no idea. We didn't have scouts in Paradise Falls, but since moving to Moonrise, I'd discovered the wonderful cookies they sold every year. I had to admit I'd blown my grocery budget once or twice on Thin Mints and Caramel deLites.

"You're thinking about cookies right now, aren't you?" Tess asked.

"I am," I admitted. "I'm hungry enough to eat a truckload."

Tess snickered and bumped her shoulder against mine. "Perks of eating for two is that you can eat all you want, and no one can say a damn thing."

"Absolutely."

"I wish I could have done this with Carlos, though." Her eyes were wistful. "He always wanted a daughter. We thought we would have more time."

This time, she was telling the truth. "That really sucks," I offered sincerely.

Tess' eyes widened then she let out a bark of laughter. "It really does suck." She beamed a smile at me. "Thank you, Lily."

"For what?"

"For not trying to make me feel better about my dead husband. I don't usually tell people because I don't want to listen to them tell me how sorry they are or whatever."

I shrugged. "People mean well."

Tess smirked. "People are stupid."

I chuckled. "That too."

She glanced over at Wells and Jeanine as they walked out of the room. "And some people are a total waste of good air."

I thought it was a bit harsh, but Tess was holding on to a secret, and it involved the Neeleys. The fact that she hadn't told me already meant it wasn't going to be something she volunteered to divulge easily or on purpose.

Andi let out a nervous giggle. I'd almost forgotten she was there.

"You know Wells Neeley?" I asked.

She nodded. "For a long time. We went to school together." She looked around as if making sure no one would overhear, then said, "He has always been a little full of himself. Wells likes to act like a self-made man, but his dad gave him the money for the dealership and," her voice dropped another decibel, "from what I've heard, he almost lost it a few years ago." She pivoted her gaze to Gail. "My husband's the loan officer at the bank."

I leaned in, and so did Tess.

"What was that between him and Pete earlier?" I asked.

She was happily stuck-in now with the gossip, and she whispered, "Oh, Wells is just acting like a big man. He wants everyone to kiss the ground he walks on."

"I've known people like him," I told her. "Ugh. Poor Jeanine."

"Oh, she's the one person he treats like gold." Andi smiled. "Don't feel too sorry for her."

Before I could ask more, Larissa gave a clap to get our attention. "Time to go, parents. Don't forget, next week we are having a fun baby shower party." Larissa had told us about it at the end of our first class, and we'd all voted to do it. "Bring your favorite snack and one gender-neutral baby gift under ten dollars in value for the white elephant exchange.

Fun or functional. It's your choice. We're going to have such a good time!"

Tess gave us a slight eye roll. Andi and I laughed.

"See you next week," I told her.

"Yep." Tess rubbed her round belly. "Same fat time, same fat channel."

CHAPTER
FIVE

Blush pink and pale green balloons on sticks decorated every corner of the birthing classroom. Rainbows of streamers were strung in scalloped waves along the ceiling, and two tables had been set up for gifts and snacks. I'd brought Ooey-Gooey Butter Cake bars, a favorite of mine since Parker had made me a batch for Valentine's Day. He'd said they were his mother's favorite, and the buttery, chewy, vanilla-y, cream-cheesy cake had lived up to the hype. So yummy. I'd modified it slightly when I made it by using lemon cake instead of vanilla, and man, it was heaven in a baking pan. The recipe, which consisted of four simple ingredients—cake mix, eggs, cream cheese, and butter—was so easy, even a kitchen disaster like me could make it. I couldn't wait until we made it for our girl.

Tess came up behind me and looked over my shoulder at the dessert table. "Oh-mer-gersh! Is that gooey butter cake? My aunt in Grand Rapids used to make that every family reunion. She'd bake two in massive sheet cake pans, and it would be the first thing we all gobbled up."

"Oh, are you from Michigan?" I asked.

Tess looked surprised for a moment, then gave a head shake. "No."

That wasn't a complete lie. There was something about Tess that I really liked, but she had a penchant for half-truths and out-and-out lies. I told myself to let it go, but *myself* refused to mind. "When did you move to Moonrise?"

She studied me for a moment. "What makes you think I'm not from around here?" Her tone was light, but there was an earnest quality to her question. She wanted an answer.

"I don't know," I told her. "There's a character to the people who were born and raised in Moonrise. My husband, Parker, is one of them. It's in the cadence of their speech, even in the way they walk. Transplants, like me, just don't have it."

Tess scratched her head and said, "You got me.

I'm not from here. I moved about six months ago from Kansas City."

"I thought you were from Fallon," Jackie said. "Or maybe I misheard you when you were talking to Wells."

Tess went total deer in the headlights. "I...no, yes, I'm from Fallon, but after I lived in Kansas City for a few years." She softly bonked her forehead with the heel of her palm. "Hormones."

Ping. Ping. Kansas City had been mostly the truth. Fallon and hormones were lies. I understood hiding a past. I'd done it, but this was getting a little bizarre.

Before I could say another word, Larissa clapped her hands to get our attention. Most of the parents had arrived, with the exception of Gail and Andi. Larissa had decorated two tables, one for snacks and the other for gifts. "I'll be right back. I left one of the games in my car."

"Cute," Tess commented. "But it's a lot of color."

"It's nice," I commented.

"We got the nursery set up this week," I heard Lizzie tell Jackie

"Oh!" Jackie exclaimed. "Do you have pictures? Show us."

A knot formed in my gut. I still needed to set up the nursery. Our house had three bedrooms. Two upstairs, including our master bedroom, and one downstairs. If the one downstairs hadn't been so small, we would have made it the master. Right now, it was Parker's home office. The second upstairs bedroom had doubled as a guest bedroom and storage for all of Parker's things that had made it from his old house. In other words, it was cluttered floor to ceiling. We'd talked about cleaning it out and getting rid of items that Parker no longer cared about, but we both worked a lot, and neither of us wanted to use up energy in our downtime cleaning the room out.

However, Buzz had brought over Journey's crib over the weekend, so Parker and I decided to tackle the cleaning soon.

Lizzie took out her phone and swiped through a foray of pictures, several of which included their son.

Tess and I went to one side of them, and I had to raise up on my tiptoes to get a look.

"Your son is a total cutie-pants," Donna cooed.

Anna chimed in, "I get the credit for him."

Lizzie snickered and shook her head, then acquiesced. "He's your Mini-me."

The toddler had dark hair and brown eyes like Anna. "Spitting image," Jackie agreed. "Adorable."

Anna grinned. "Thank you."

Then, the nursery came up. "We went with coral, salmon, and flamingo for the color scheme."

All I saw was a lot of variations on pink.

"Cute," Tess muttered in my ear. "But it's a lot of pink."

I cracked a smile because I'd been thinking the same thing.

Tess and I were both having girls as well, but I planned to go with more neutral colors of yellows and teals, with touches of pink and blue. My best friend Hazel loved pink, but I was never a pink kind of girl. Still, the place was adorable.

Jeanine came over and said, "I love it, Lizzie."

Jackie took a few steps back and then looked around. Her brows knitted together, and she looked dismayed. Parker had joined Sal and Gail over by the cubbies. The three of them were deep in commiseration. But I didn't see Pete anywhere, or Wells, for that matter.

Tess dipped down and bumped her shoulder against mine. "Be right back. Call of nature."

Pete walked in, and Jackie went over to him. I heard Jackie whisper, "Where have you been? I swear, Pete, you better tell him this is over. No more."

Interesting. My ears perked up for more. Other than, "It's done," Pete didn't say any more.

Eeep. Who did he need to end something with? Wells? I didn't think Pete was gay or bisexual, but it could've been an affair. Gosh. How awful for Jackie if that was the case? No wonder she'd been off tonight.

"Lils." Parker waved me over, so I excused myself from the moms' group to join him.

I took his hand when he held it out. "What's up, buttercup?"

My guy's eyes were alight with excitement. "Sal is interested in adopting Sparrow."

My heart melted. Sparrow was a pit bull-basset hound and probably a bit of mutt, and she was the goofiest, sweetest pupper, but she also had some major health problems, including diabetes. Her medical needs made her a hard sell to adoptees. She'd been with us for a little over a year now. "That's amazing," I told Sal. "She is the goodest girl."

He grinned. "I saw her on your website, and Donna and I fell in love instantly."

I didn't want to dissuade them from applying for

her, but I also wanted to make sure they knew what they were getting into. "Did you read her bio?"

He gave me a knowing nod. "I'm a type one diabetic." He lifted up the bottom of his shirt to show me his insulin pump. "I was diagnosed at fourteen. Sparrow would be in good hands."

Tears pooled in my eyes. "I can't wait for you to meet her."

"Come by tomorrow," Parker told him.

Gail said, "We're still on tomorrow, too, right?"

"Oh, right!" I dabbed at my eyes with the pads of my thumbs.

Gail and Andi had passed the foster background check with flying colors, and Parker had done the home visit on Sunday. They had a lovely ranch-style house and a nice-sized fenced-in backyard that was perfect for a large dog. I'd planned to introduce them to three of our older rescues that I thought would be a perfect fit.

Lizzie's laugh as she talked with Donna and Andi drew my attention, but several people were missing. Where was Tess?

Jeanine came into the room, her brow wrinkled as she wrung her hands. I went to her.

"Are you okay?"

"I can't find Wells," she said. "I thought he went

to the bathroom, but I just checked and couldn't find him."

"Did you try calling his phone?"

"We put our phones in the cubbies. I went to the parking lot, and our car is still here." Jeanine fretted. "I'm worried."

"Would he leave you here without telling you he was going somewhere?"

"No." She scratched the crown of her head. Her voice was tight with stress. "He wouldn't. I only looked because I couldn't think of anything else. I'm worried something happened to him."

"Do you have any reason to think something bad would happen to him?"

"No." *Ping.* "I'm just being overly sensitive, probably."

I waved my hand at Parker, gesturing for him to come over. When he got there, I said, "Wells is missing."

"Missing?"

"Maybe it's a prank," Gail said. "Wells might be messing with you."

"He wouldn't do that," Jeanine denied. "Something's wrong. I know it is." She was verging on hysteria but, for some reason, I didn't think it was unwarranted.

Larissa came back into the room, game in hand. "Has anyone seen Trevor?" She looked discombobulated but gathered her wits when she noticed the state Jeanine was in. "Did something happen? Where is everyone?"

I grimaced. "I'm not sure, but Jeanine is worried about Wells. She can't find him."

"I'll check to see if his phone is still here. Maybe he took it with him." She moved quickly to the box and pulled out her purse and a sweater. "It's still here." She held out the phone then her face paled. She put her hand to her mouth and muttered, "You're a dead man."

I looked at the fretting blonde. "What?" I asked.

"That's what the message on his screen says," Jeanine said shrilly. She held it out for all of us to see.

CHAPTER
SIX

Jeanine, her expression stunned, held out the phone to the room. We all looked at the message sitting on Wells' lock screen. The caller was listed as "Unknown."

"That has to be a joke, right?" Sal asked.

Pete shook his head, and Jackie moved close and linked her arm with his. The conversation I'd overheard earlier between the couple was strange and suspect. And before I could stop myself, I blurted out, "Do you know where Wells is?"

Jackie's eyes went wide before narrowing at me. Pete opened his mouth as if he would speak, but Jackie glared at me and said, "Why would Pete know where Wells is?"

Her question stopped Pete from answering. I'd

eavesdropped from across the room. That would be difficult to explain to a roomful of humans, so I didn't even try. Instead, I punted. "Pete left and returned just a little while ago," I explained to Jackie. "I thought he might've run into Wells in the center somewhere."

"He didn't," Jackie said.

"I didn't see him either," Larissa added.

Ping. Ping. Crap. Why was *she* lying? As far as I knew, other than the connection through this class, Larissa and Wells had no ties. Moonrise was a small town, but that didn't mean everyone knew everyone. Heck, until this class, I hadn't met anyone in our group.

Jeanine started toward the door.

"Where are you going?" Larissa asked.

The blonde woman gave her an "are you stupid?" stare. "I'm going to find my husband." The "duh" was implied.

Anna stood behind Lizzie and rubbed her back. Lizzie said, "We're going with you."

"Us too," I told Jeanine.

She gave me a grateful nod.

"We'll all go," Larissa said, to which the rest of the parents agreed.

We filed out of the classroom and past the

clanking of weights and sweaty gym rats as a group. We checked every open door on the upstairs level, including the bathrooms, and couldn't find any sign of Wells. We went down the stairs like a pregnant parade with a frantic Jeanine leading the pack. We must've looked like mothers—and fathers—on a mission because several people passing by gave us a wide berth.

"Did anyone check the pool?" Lizzie asked. She walked over to the glass wall and peered through. I'd gone swimming with Nadine a couple of times, so I knew it had an Olympic-sized pool on one side of the aquatic center and a giant indoor water slide and a shallow kiddie pool in the other half of the room. The pool area was dimly lit, but the rest of the enormous room was dark.

"Do you see anything?" Jeanine asked.

"I think so," Lizzie told her. "Someone is moving over on the far end of the pool."

Jeanine rushed over and smacked her palm against the laminated glass wall multiple times, her ring making a clunk sound that grew louder with every hit. "Wells!" she shouted. "Wells!" The glass had an air gap between the panes, and it kept the pool noise from polluting the lobby and vice versa. Her pounding wouldn't get his attention.

I pressed my face to the glass. As a human, I couldn't see much more than the worried wife could through the clear wall, but my animal's night vision was better than mine. I cupped my hands around my eyes as if blocking out the light and let my cougar slip into my gaze.

It took a second for the night vision to settle in, but it didn't take me long to recognize the person near the back of the pool.

It was Tess Danvers, my class buddy. A slight glow was on her cheek as if she had a phone to her face. She knelt down and rifled through a large dark bag. What was she doing? She took something from the bag. Was that...yes, wow, it was a fistful of cash. She tucked it back in before looking around. Her gaze darted around the room, and she looked startled when she saw all of us pressed up against the wall. Or maybe it was my eyes. Either way, she grabbed the bag and bolted toward the back of the room.

Crap. I pulled back my cougar and turned to Parker.

He mouthed, "Wells?"

I shook my head. I had no idea what Tess was doing in the locked area, but I hadn't seen Wells.

"We need to get inside," Parker said.

"The locker rooms are the only way in and out from this side," Larissa informed us.

Andi went to the door of the men's side. "Locked."

Unfortunately, all the doors were locked, and there was a sign that said, "Aquatic Center closed Wednesday Night."

Then how had Tess found her way inside? "Larissa, go find someone with a key, please."

The doula shoved her hand in her pocket, then shook her head. She turned on her heel and jogged to the front desk.

Soon, Larissa hustled back with a young man with curly hair and cheek acne trailing behind. "Come on," she snapped.

The kid's doughy eyes flashed irritation as he moved past her to the door for the men's locker room. "I'm not supposed to let anyone in when the pool is closed."

Our instructor's wild eyes made her appear unhinged. "Shut up, Billy, and open the door."

The curly-headed kid made a noise of dissent before nodding his head. His keys jangled as he opened the door.

"Why is the pool closed?" I asked Billy.

"Repairs and cleaning," he replied as he stepped out of the way.

Jeanine was the first person through the door. As a group, we navigated past lockers, the shower area, and out the door on the other side. The stringent scent of chlorine and stale, damp air hit me as we entered the pool area.

"Wells!" Jeanine shouted again.

I examined the room and didn't see Tess or the bag of money. There was an emergency exit on the opposite wall.

A scream tore from Jeanine's mouth as the lights flipped on, illuminating the entire area. Her face was contorted in horror.

A blond man was floating face down in the pool and blood blossomed in the water around his head. I didn't need to see his face to know it was Wells Neeley.

Parker let go of my hand, ran to the end of the pool, and jumped in, shoes and all. He was the first to Wells.

"Call nine-one-one," I ordered Billy. He was in an age group that was rarely without their phone.

He fished his phone from his back pocket and did as he was told, but when the operator asked him how she could help, he froze. He stared at me, and I realized he was in shock. I took the phone from him.

"This is Lily Mason. We need an ambulance and the police at the community center pool."

"Lily," the woman said. I recognized her voice as Maggie Winters, an operator I'd talked to a few times in person since the time I'd found a murdered man in his own house. "Please don't tell me you found another body."

I glanced over at Parker, who was lifting Wells from the pool with the help of Gail, Pete, and Sal. He gave me a slight head shake.

I winced. "You might want to send the coroner too."

CHAPTER
SEVEN

Police cordoned off the entire aquatic center as we sat in the front lobby, waiting to be questioned.

"I don't understand," Andi said. "How does something like this happen?"

"He probably slipped and fell," Sal offered hopefully.

"But what was he doing by the pool in the first place?" Lizzie asked.

That was the million-dollar question, wasn't it? Or, in this case, however much money had been in the satchel Tess had taken. I hadn't said anything about seeing her to the other parents, but I planned to tell Bobby Morris the minute he stopped glowering at me.

"Lily," he called, beckoning me over.

I'd been squeezing Parker's hand so hard his fingers had turned red. I winced. "Sorry."

"Do you want me to go with you?"

I nodded. "I do, but Bobby's not going to let you." He'd already said he would talk to us one at a time. "I'll be fine." I leaned my head against his shoulder briefly.

"Lily!" Bobby said more sharply.

I sighed. "I'll be back." I kissed Parker, then walked over to the waiting sheriff. I gave him a "welp, here we are again" look.

Bobby shook his head. "You really are a body magnet."

"I wish people would quit saying that."

"Then quit being around every time a body is discovered."

"I can't help it."

"Like I said." He blew out a low whistle. "Body magnet."

"Aren't you a little late to be out, Sheriff? I thought you kept bankers' hours now that you were the head man in charge."

"If someone dies under suspicious circumstances, I need to be on top of it from the beginning."

"And reelection is coming up soon," I pointed out.

He shook his head, but he didn't deny it.

"Don't worry, Bobby, I mean, Sheriff Morris. You have my vote."

The corner of his mouth tugged up into a crooked smile. "Thanks, Lily."

As a black man in a small town, Bobby had an uphill climb to get the support he needed for a campaign, and I knew it wasn't something he could easily dismiss when it came to the politics of the job. We lived in the twenty-first century, but that didn't stop twentieth-century thinking.

I gave him a serious look. "You've been great for this town. No one can deny it."

"I appreciate you saying so," he told me. "So, what did you see that everyone else missed." The quirk at the corner of his mouth verged on a full smile. "Unless your pregnancy has muddled your brain."

I scoffed. "Not even." Bobby had let me help in a prior investigation that involved the old sheriff and corruption. On top of that, Sheriff Avery had tried to railroad my uncle Buzz for a murder. Good riddance to bad rubbish. "I'm sharp as a tack."

"Give me the goods."

I wasn't sure what was relevant, but no matter how much I liked Tess, I couldn't *not* report that she was by the pool with a bag of money. I had friends I'd lie for, but she wasn't one of them.

"You need to find Tess Danvers," I told him quietly. "I saw her by the pool before we found Wells Neeley. And I'm not saying she killed him, only that she knows something. And there was a duffle bag on the ground. I saw her take a handful of cash out. I don't know if the rest was full of more cash, clothes, or something else, but when she ran out the back, she took the bag with her."

"Cripes, Lily." Bobby shook his head. "You could've led with all that."

"I didn't want to say anything in front of the other parents. Tess is six months pregnant, and Wells was a jerk. Maybe he did something that provoked her."

"Are you setting up a not-guilty-by-reason-of-hormone-insanity defense for her already?"

I rolled my eyes. "How did these jokes go over when your wife was pregnant with your sons."

He let out a faint chuckle. "About as well as they're going over now."

I peered up at him. "So, you know better."

"Uh-yep." He pulled his shoulders back,

straightening his posture. "Is there anything else I should know?"

"Several people in the class were out and about in the community center when Wells disappeared, and one or two of them didn't care for the man."

He arched a thick brow. "Like who?"

I casually glanced at Pete and Jackie Reynolds, and quietly said, "Pete works for Wells, and they have butted heads a few times."

"Interesting." Bobby turned so that his back was to the birthing class group. "Anyone else?"

"Jackie, his wife, isn't a fan. I don't remember her leaving the room, but I was busy drooling over the snacks."

"Did you notice anyone else that had slipped out?"

I chewed the side of my lip as I tried to remember where everyone was located. "Larissa Merriweather, our teacher. She came back looking upset. Then there's Trevor, Larissa's assistant. He isn't here. I haven't seen him at all tonight."

"Tell me what happened when you went inside."

"Jeanine led the way after Billy opened the door. The lights came on when we went inside, and then Jeanine screamed. Wells was face down. Blood in the pool. Parker jumped in and, with some help, got him out. He wasn't breathing, and he didn't have a pulse. Anna, a certified med tech, performed CPR while Larissa retrieved the automated external defibrillator, but he couldn't be revived."

"Who turned on the lights?"

"I don't know," I replied. "I guess I assumed they were automatic and motion-based."

"If that were the case, wouldn't the lights have come on when you saw Tess in there?"

I raised both brows. "Interesting. Good observation."

"I *am* good at my job," he said plainly. "I was crime-busting long before you came to Moonrise."

"Oh." I snapped my fingers. "I almost forgot. Several weeks ago, I saw Wells in the park in an argument with someone."

"You didn't see who?" Bobby asked.

"Nah. He had on a jogging suit and a stocking cap. Talk to Nadine. She was there and stopped the fight from escalating. It didn't last long, and no one was hurt, but it might be something."

"Thanks." He tucked his thumb in his pocket. "I'll call you if I have any more questions. Once I talk to Parker, you two can go."

"We're not suspects, huh?"

"If you ever decide to kill someone, I'm sure of

two things: they will probably deserve it, and no one will ever find the body." He shook his head. "This is too sloppy to be your work."

"You say the nicest things." I smirked. "Give my regards to Macy and the boys."

Bobby tipped his head to me. "Will do." He gestured for Parker. "We'll talk soon, I'm sure."

Parker and I passed by each other, our fingers brushing, and I went and sat down next to Jackie and Andi.

"I can't believe this is happening," Jackie muttered.

"Does this mean the party is canceled?" Andi sniffed.

Jackie snapped, "Don't be stupid!"

Andi teared up. "I want to go home. I just want to go home." She got up and went to Gail. He put his arms around her in a protective hug.

"Something like this is overwhelming," I told Jackie. "Don't take Andi personally. She's upset."

"As we all are," Jackie said tersely. Her knee bounced as she watched Pete talking with Deputy Gary Hall. Hall had been on the job for a few years, and according to Nadine, he'd become a good investigator. He'd been a new deputy when I'd met the man. He'd tried to arrest Parker and pulled his weapon on me. In other words, he'd made a terrible first impression.

Gary peered over at Jackie and me, and when his eyes met mine, he gave me a genial nod.

I couldn't stop thinking about Tess. Could she be Wells' killer? Absolutely. Pregnant or not, anyone could be driven to murder, given the right circumstances. But I also thought a few others had opportunity and maybe more motive. Of course, I hadn't found any of them with their hand in a bag of cash near the dead guy in the pool.

After a few moments of silence, Jackie said, "I'm sorry, Lily. You didn't deserve that." She shook her head. "Neither did Andi."

"It's okay. It's all such a shock."

"It really is." She leaned forward and rested her elbows on her knees. Her dark hair fell over her eyes. "I can't believe this is happening."

"Poor Jeanine."

Jackie scoffed. Her shoulders slumped forward. "I'm being a real witch."

I knew some real witches, but I knew Jackie was talking about the B kind. "It's okay. I know Pete worked for Wells, and you're Jeanine's cousin, but were you all close?"

"Jeanine and I used to be," Jackie said. "I was

even friends with Wells when we were all younger, but he's treated Pete badly." She shook her head. "He did. He and Wells were working things out."

"I don't mean to be blunt, but it didn't look like it last week. Wells got harsh with him."

She peered at me, her mouth contorting into a scowl. "What are you trying to say?"

"Nothing," I told her. "It's just an observation."

She got up from the bench and said, "Keep your observations to yourself."

Too late, I thought. I'd already told Bobby to look at them.

Stylish even in jeans, a red sweater, and low-heeled boots, Reggie arrived through the front doors of the community center. She had her black hair back in a sleek bun—her work-do. She carried a brown duffel with the word "Coroner" written across the side. The police on the scene knew who she was and didn't stop her as she approached.

I stood up, and Reggie's hard expression immediately looked relieved.

"Oh, Lily." She put her bag down and took my hand when I met her in the middle of the lobby. "Are you feeling okay?"

"Fine," I told her.

"You should've called me."

"I knew you'd be coming. Besides, my phone is back up in the room. The sheriff wouldn't let anyone leave this area until he gave the okay, so I couldn't have called."

She peered around the room. The light in the lobby cast a yellow glow, making her dark brown eyes look wolfish. "Is Nadine here?"

"No." I sighed. "She's not on duty tonight, but Bobby's here. He's handling the case."

"Who's the deceased?" Reggie asked curiously. "Must be someone important if Bobby is running point."

"I don't know about important..." It dawned on me that I didn't know much about Wells other than the fact that he owned a car dealership, rubbed people the wrong way, and was a bit of a jerk. Even so, he'd had people who loved him. I glanced over at Jeanine, who was still with the paramedics. She'd been inconsolable after Wells had been pronounced dead on the scene. "His name is Wells Neely. He owns Moonrise Motors here in town."

Reggie's chin dropped.

"Do you know him?"

"Not to see him," she whispered. "But he's an alderman in town. He recently put forward an agenda to vote on whether or not the sheriff's department should be moved out of town limits and the police force should be disbanded."

"What would we do for law enforcement?"

"He suggested that we outsource officers who only come in when needed."

"For what reason?"

"Because he's an idiot." Reggie's gaze pivoted past me. "I better get in there."

"Keep me up to date."

"Never." She tapped her nose and winked. "See you for lunch at the diner tomorrow."

"Perfect."

Parker finished up with Bobby and made his way back to me. "Let's go get our stuff."

"Are we allowed to go back upstairs?"

"I'm not sure." He frowned. "Bobby said we could go, but I didn't think to ask."

Pete sullenly stalked off after Deputy Hall finished with him. I waved at the young officer to get his attention.

He waved and walked over. "Hey, Ms. Mason," he greeted. "Mr. Holden."

"Hi, Deputy Hall." It was all very formal but friendly. "Can we go upstairs and get our things from the classroom?"

He nodded. "I don't see why not."

"Great. We're ready to get out of here."

"I don't blame you." He looked down at my stomach. "Congratulations."

"Thanks."

Parker took my hand and tugged me in the direction of the stairs. I'd forgiven Hall, but my guy hadn't been able to get past the image of the officer holding me at gunpoint. I doubted he ever would.

On our way up the stairs, a man bounded down the steps two at a time. He had on a black nylon jacket and a pair of matching track pants as he passed us. He lifted his head as he grunted out a quick "pardon" before continuing down.

It was Trevor Peters, Larissa's assistant. Tess seemed like the logical suspect, but I couldn't help but wonder where Trevor had been tonight when Wells was killed.

CHAPTER
EIGHT

Early the next day, baby girl Knowles was doing summersaults in my belly as I drove slightly above the speed limit to The Cat's Meow diner. I'd just finished a half-day at Petry's Pet Clinic, and in an hour, Parker and I were meeting with Gail and Andi to introduce them to potential foster babies, along with Sal and Donna coming by to see Sparrow.

But first, lunch. Nadine and Reggie were meeting me for a quick bite and to dish about the night before. I was ten minutes early, so I texted the ladies after I parked Martha around the back by Buzz's car.

"Buzz," Freda hollered when I walked through the front door of the restaurant. "We're going to need a triple-decker cheeseburger with extra jalapenos, chili cheese fries, an order of fried mush-rooms, and a side salad with extra Ranch dressing." She smiled at me. "Order is on the way, Lily. I'll get you a large glass of milk and some water."

I grinned. "Thanks, Freda. You take real good care of me."

"That's why they pay me the big bucks." She pinned me with a more serious gaze. "Are you feeling okay? You're not overdoing it, are you?"

"I'm feeling pretty good," I told her. "Apparently, I'm still in the nesting phase, so I have lots of energy."

"Good times," she said fondly. "I remember that month when I was pregnant with Lacy. I cleaned my house from top to bottom in a week, set up the nurs-ery, and still managed to put in a forty-hour week at work. It was better than speed."

"I haven't set up the nursery yet." I felt a twinge of panic, but we still had a few months, right? What was the rush? "Is that something I'm supposed to do now?"

Freda tilted her head at me. "Only if you feel up to it. But keep in mind, once you're late into the seventh month, you might not feel like or be able to do a bunch of heavy lifting and painting. I was exhausted all the time and uncomfortable, and it didn't help that I couldn't see my feet anymore. Do it while you can, Lily. The sixth month is kind of God's way of getting you off your butt to prepare your home for the new kiddo."

"Thanks for the advice."

"Anytime." Freda patted her apron pocket then went back to the kitchen.

My shoulders sagged as I sat in a booth near the back by a window. At least we had a crib—*thank you, Nadine and Buzz*. That was something, right?

Freda set a tall glass of milk down in front of me. I wrinkled my nose. "This would be better if it was full of soda."

"And have Buzz fire me?" She slid the glass closer. "No, thank you. Drink up, buttercup. Your baby is sapping all the calcium from your bones. You need the extra dose."

We'd covered calcium in the nutrition part of the birthing classes, and I'd learned that fetuses do not, in fact, take calcium from a mother's bones or teeth. It's an old wives' tale. However, it was important to up your calcium during pregnancy to prevent other problems like preeclampsia, which could be dangerous for me and the little kickboxer in my belly.

Extra protein was also a must. Larissa had

recommended that we start the day with two eggs and call them our protein pills. They were also high in B vitamins, along with A, D, E, and K, and a slew of other minerals. I was surprised when I found out that the amount covered up to thirty percent of our daily vitamin needs. Of course, I quadrupled my egg intake because of my physiological differences.

Lately, I'd been blaming Smooshie and Elvis for all my egg toots. Both of them had broad shoulders and could take the burden. Parker knew better, of course, but he humored me all the same. He was good like that.

Buzz, striking with his cinnamon-red hair, a little darker than mine, strolled out of the kitchen carrying two plates piled high with lunch. The grilled meat scent of the triple burger made my mouth water.

"Here you go." He put them down in front of me and grinned.

"Nadine and Reggie are joining me." I stared at the hot and tempting plates of food. "I should wait for them, right?"

"Eat," Buzz insisted. "You look tired. Why don't you put your feet up on the bench?"

I kicked my short legs up. "They don't reach."

"I'll get you a vegetable crate to put under the table."

"I don't want to put you out!"

He set his hand on my shoulder and gave it a squeeze. "You're my family, Lily. The little sister I never had."

I snorted. "Or wanted."

"I haven't regretted a minute since the day you walked into my diner asking for Daniel Mason."

I loved the way he worried about me. I hadn't even known Buzz existed until after Danny's death. I'd grown up thinking that I had no other family. Thanks to my friend Hazel, I'd discovered my dad had a brother. Daniel Mason. My dad had named my brother for him. It turned out that Buzz had been in love with my mother, but Dad had caught the mating scent for her. The realization that he couldn't be with her had driven him away from Paradise Falls, and that's when he'd become what we in the shifter world called an integrator.

I'd walked into the place not knowing if Buzz would even want to know me. He had looked very much like my father and brother, with coppery-cinnamon hair and a thick beard, tall and well-muscled. He'd been wearing a white apron around his waist, and he'd had on a black T-shirt and blue jeans. Looking at him now in basically the same clothes made me smile. It was hard to believe it had been almost five years ago. Wow.

My showing up had thrown a real monkey wrench in his plans to avoid attachment. He'd fallen in love with Nadine before my arrival, but I think his decision to stay and make the relationship work had a lot to do with Parker and me. Parker had accepted me, cougar and all. It had given Buzz hope that Nadine might do the same. Luckily, with a little time, she had.

I smiled at Buzz. "You're the big brother I always wanted."

He took a towel from his apron and flapped it at me. "Hush now. You're gonna make an old man cry."

I laughed when I heard, "If you're old, then I must be a flippin' dinosaur." I recognized Pearl Dixon's voice immediately. Pearl's hair was fluffy and blue. The younger Dixon sister loved playing with color. She'd been a Vegas showgirl in her heyday, and I think the color was her way of saying, 'I'm still here.' I wanted to be her when I grew up. Her sister Opal, the more serious of the two, was right behind her, letting all her natural white hair shine. They ate their lunch at The Cat's Meow every day. I'd also met them on my first day in

Moonrise, and over the years, they'd become family as well.

"Pearl, you're a darn fossil," Opal teased her younger sister.

"And what does that make you?" Pearl asked.

"Another darn fossil." Opal cackled. "But I own it." Her gray-blue eyes brightened when she looked at me. "Lily! How is that baby of ours doing? She cooking okay?"

I had told the Dixons about having a girl recently, and the pair of them had flipped their lids with excitement.

"She's slow-basting," I told her. "She'll be nice and juicy in a few months."

Pearl chuckled. "I can't wait to meet her. She'll have two grannies who plan to spoil her rotten."

Hearing Pearl say grannies made me tear up.

Opal gave her sister a light smack. "You made her cry, dummy."

"It's happy tears," I told them. "Really happy tears."

The sisters took a seat at their regular booth near the door.

Buzz tapped the table. "Eat."

"I'm eating." I moved the burger plate until it was right in front of me and I could lean over it. My growing tummy had become a catch-all for any and all food drippings. I still had three months and some change to go, and I didn't want to invest in a new wardrobe every week because all my clothes were stained. I grabbed the burger. "See." I took a bite."

"Good. You know, if you or that little niece of mine need anything, all you have to do is ask. I'd move the moon for you."

After I swallowed, I said, "I know you would." My fondness for my uncle grew every day. Sometimes, he reminded me so much of my dad, and it was more comfort than pain.

"So, have you given more thought to upgrading your vehicle?" he asked.

"Smooooth," I told him. "Did Parker tell you to poke me?" I took a huge bite of my burger, the juices running down the sides of my mouth. *"Iaammmm nawtgettin brid awf marsha,"* I told him as I chewed the delicious combination of seasoned ground beef, smoky bacon, gooey cheese, pickles, tomato, and lettuce on a sesame seed bun.

Buzz rolled his eyes. "No one's saying you should get rid of Martha."

"Goood." I devoured the last of it. "Because she's my ride or die, and I'm riding her until she dies."

"She has died several times," Buzz countered.

"One of these days, Greer won't be able to put her back together."

"When that day comes, I'll talk about a new vehicle." I waved a fry at him. "*Unpill ben.*"

Buzz sighed and shook his head. "You need something reliable."

I waited until my mouth was empty to speak again. "You're stressing me and the baby out." I cradled my stomach for emphasis.

"Fine." Buzz threw his hands up and walked away. "But when you're ready to be a grown-up, let me know."

The door to the diner repeatedly opened and closed as customers arrived for lunch. Nadine and Reggie would be arriving anytime, and with the current conversation, I was on Team The-Sooner-The-Better.

"I am a grown-up," I mumbled. A grown-up pregnant woman with a whole life that included a husband, a job, a house, and a whole slew of responsibilities. Having a new SUV wouldn't change my grown-up status. "So there," I added pithily before I settled back into my meal.

Pete sat at the counter across from my booth. He inclined his head to me. "Looks good," he observed as he stared at my plates of food. "How many are you eating for?"

I gave him a sideways glance and tried not to growl.

"Kidding," he said. "It's hard work building a whole 'nother human being."

I gestured with my half-eaten burger. "Are you picking up lunch for Jackie?"

"No," he answered. "The doctor has her on a low-sodium, low-carb diet because her blood pressure was really high at our visit today. He's worried about preeclampsia."

I could imagine. "Could the hypertension be stress related?" After all, the night before would've been enough to make Buddha lose his Zen.

"It might be, which is why he wants her to try the diet and take it easy for a few days."

"So, no cake then, huh? Bummer." I was as sympathetic as the next person, but my growing child wanted freaking cake.

Pete frowned. "She'd kill me if she knew I was indulging in a greasy burger, but I need it today."

"Not greasy," Buzz corrected from the kitchen window. "Juicy."

Pete chuckled. "Greasy or juicy, it's all off-limits to her." He shrugged. "Our little secret."

I grabbed a napkin and wiped burger drippings from my chin. "What's Jackie doing this morning?" It wasn't quite noon yet, so it was technically still morning. "I mean, is she okay after last night? She was really upset."

"Someone we know died," Pete protested. The question had made him defensive. "It was a terrible thing to witness."

I nodded. "I know. I was there."

His eyes widened and then narrowed as he grimaced. "Of course. Yep. Are you doing okay?"

I looked at the mounds of food in front of me. "I still have my appetite."

That made Pete laugh. "That's something, I suppose."

Pete was a nice guy. I liked him, even if he was on my top-five list for murder.

"Are you eating alone?"

"No," I said. "I have friends joining me." A tap at the window startled me. I looked over and Nadine and Reggie were standing just outside. They waved and headed to the door. I gestured with my thumb. "There they are now."

"Bacon cheeseburger, extra mayo," Freda set a to-go bag in front of Pete on the counter. "That'll be eight-fifty."

Pete stood up and took his wallet from his back pocket. He gave me a quick nod. "I'll let you get back to your lunch."

"Enjoy the burger," I told him then turned my excited gaze to my friends. They were both smiling and shaking their heads as they slid into the other side of the booth.

"Way to start without us," Nadine ribbed me. "Although, you probably have enough for everyone."

When she reached out her hand to steal one of my fries, I knocked it away.

"Oooh," she crooned. "Catlike reflexes."

"Har har." I rolled my eyes, but I couldn't help but smile. "I'm so glad you all are here."

"Me too," Reggie said. "I have so much to tell you about—"

I cut her off by saying, "How would you all like to come over this weekend and help me paint the nursery?"

Nadine bounced in her seat. "Yes, definitely. I'm in."

"I'm in too," Reggie added. "But I figured you'd want to know—"

I held up my finger then turned to the departing Pete. "See you next week at birthing class. Tell Jackie hello from me."

"If they don't shut it down." He gave me a tight smile. "Have a good day, Lily."

Reggie's mouth had formed a small 'o'. "Got it," she said. "No talking in front of witnesses."

"Or suspects," I added.

"Really?" Nadine scooted forward and whispered, "Why do you say that?"

"Have you read the report?"

"It's my day off," she said. "I go in tomorrow, but when you called to get the Moonrise Murder Club together, I wasn't going to miss it. But you all are going to have to fill me in on the nitty-gritty."

"First things first," I told them. "Reggie, do you know the cause of death?" Blunt force head trauma or drowning was the most obvious, but obvious wasn't always the right answer.

"He had a penetrating head wound," she shared.

Nadine scrunched her face. "Like a knife to the skull?"

Reggie shook her head. "Like a bullet. A twenty-two-caliber bullet that I found inside his head."

"A bullet?" Now I scooted forward. My belly made it difficult, but I succeeded. "I didn't hear a gunshot. Of course, I was upstairs and the pool is on the first floor behind a wall of glass, but the place isn't soundproof."

"A silencer," Nadine added. "Someone could've used a silencer to keep the noise down. Now tell me everything before I arrest the both of you for obstruction of justice."

I giggled. "Wells Neeley was found dead at the indoor community pool last night."

Nadine nodded. "You told me that last night. Tell me all the stuff you *didn't* tell me."

I lowered my voice. "This is the part that I told Bobby and nobody else."

"Not even Parker?" Reggie looked surprised.

I scoffed. "Parker isn't nobody."

"Gotcha," she said. "Tell us the rest."

"Tess Danvers was standing by the pool taking cash out of a duffel bag. I saw her plain as the nose on your face." I chomped a fry. "When she saw us through the glass, she took off. I suspect out the emergency exit, but I don't know for sure."

"Wow," Nadine mouthed. "Isn't that the mom you're fond of in your class?"

"Yep." I shifted my butt because my right hip started to hurt. "But I don't really know her all that well. She's extremely gifted with secrets. I get a lot of half-truths from her. I knew she was hiding something, but I thought it had to do with a past that she wanted to put behind her. I know all about reinventing yourself, so I didn't pry."

"Cuh-razy," Reggie said.

"Banana-cakes," Nadine agreed. "And you told Bobby all this?"

"I had to." It didn't mean I felt good about it. I wanted Tess to be innocent. "Do you think she got picked up yet?"

Nadine shook her head. "Nope. That, I would've heard about."

Buzz came to the table with an empty wooden fruit crate. He set it on the floor and toed it under the table. "For your feet," he told me. After, he gently grasped the back of Nadine's hair and tugged her head back as he kissed her in a way that guaranteed my burger was well done. It was sizzling.

"Keep it PG," I groaned. "Baby on board."

Buzz chuckled against Nadine's lips then gave her a final peck on the lips. "Love you."

"Love you more," she said breathlessly.

"If that's on the menu, I'll take two to go," Pearl announced. Several customers laughed, including me.

Nadine was flushed, but she didn't look embarrassed. "I'll take several to go as well."

Buzz grinned. "What can I get you ladies for lunch?"

"What's the soup of the day?" Reggie inquired.

"Chicken tortilla with a mix of beans. It's a little spicy but delicious."

"That sounds wonderful. I'll take that with sourdough toast."

"Got it," Buzz told Reggie. "And you, babe?" he asked Nadine.

"Babe wanted a burger when she arrived, but after hearing about the soup, I've changed my mind."

Buzz kissed her again. "As long as you never change your mind about me."

Nadine laughed. "Never."

When Buzz walked away, Reggie and I both pinned Nadine with a stare.

"What's up, *babe*?" I asked.

Nadine giggled. "It's like we're in a second honeymoon phase. He can't get enough of me, and I *definitely* can't get enough of him."

"I know that feeling all too well," I said. I wanted Parker all the time. He was the love of my life, and I never knew what that phrase meant until I met him.

"You guys, me too," Reggie injected. "Greer is such a good lover. Caring, responsive to my needs, and damn, the man knows how to coax multiple orgasms from me."

Nadine pivoted to face our friend while I tried not to cringe. I loved hearing she was happy, in love, and had a life full of sexy time, but Greer was my father-in-law now and it felt weird to hear about his prowess as a lover.

"Do go on," Nadine encouraged.

My phone rang, saving me from the discomfort of more sex stories about Parker's dad. The number was unknown. The threat that Wells had gotten was from an unknown number. Curious, I answered the call. "Hello."

"Lily," a woman said. "I need your help."

"Tess?"

"Yes, it's me." There was a couple seconds' pause, then Tess said, "Can we meet?"

Nadine and Reggie were fully focused on me now.

"Yes," I answered Tess. "Come to The Cat's Meow."

CHAPTER
NINE

I'd told Tess to park around in the back of the diner and text me when she was at the service door. I'd let her in and the two of us could talk privately in Buzz's office. By some minor miracle, I'd convinced Nadine not to call out the S.W.A.T team. A bit of an exaggeration, but it had taken a little negotiation for her to delay calling Bobby.

"You know I have truth mojo," I told her. "If I can get Tess alone and ask her some direct questions, I might be able to get answers that *you* couldn't get."

"It's not a good idea," Nadine had countered. "She might be dangerous."

"I've been known to be dangerous as well," I countered. "Besides, Buzz and you will be right outside the door. When I'm done talking with Tess, you can take her in."

"As simple as that?" She raised a skeptical brow.

"Simpler," I assured her.

Eagerly, Reggie rubbed her long, slender hands together. "What do I get to do?"

"Enable Lily, apparently." Nadine let out a defeated sigh. "Fine. We'll do this your way, but Buzz is going to use them super ears of his to listen in, and if he hears one hinky thing, we're coming in."

"Absolutely." I slashed my hand in a movement that signaled my agreement. "I'm not going to risk me or the baby. I just have a gut feeling about Tess."

Nadine's gaze narrowed. "That she's a liar-liar-pants-on-fire?"

"Yes, that. But being a liar doesn't mean she's a murderer." My phone dinged. I saw a text that said, *I'm here.*

"Okay, you guys get out of sight. I'm going to go let her in." Buzz, Reggie, and Nadine filed into the kitchen. I went to the back door once they were out of sight and unlocked it.

Tess, wearing gray sweatpants, an oversized turquoise hoodie, and black running shoes, stood outside the door with a hang-dog look on her face. Her bloodshot eyes and the dark circles underneath told me she hadn't slept. Her white Suburban was parked next to Martha, making my truck look tiny.

"Come in," I said.

Tess peered over my head. "Is anyone around?"

"No." Not a complete lie. "Buzz's office is open, and there's no one in there."

Finally, the desperate woman walked inside. I led her into Buzz's office. I put myself between her and the door. Not to stop her if she made a break for it, but so I would have access to an escape route in case she had a gun and tried to attack me.

"What help do you need?" I asked straight away.

"You think I murdered Wells," she stated.

"I don't know *what* I think." I rubbed a spot over my brow that had started to throb. I leaned into my witch mojo. "Did you kill him?"

"No."

My truth meter was radio silence. Tess wasn't lying.

"What were you doing by the pool last night?"

"I can't tell you."

"What about the money in the bag?"

Her eyes bulged. "How did you..."

"I saw you last night. You had a wad of cash in your hand."

"It was too dark for you to see me," Tess said.

She glared at me. "Are you the reason the cops want me? Did you tell them you saw me?"

"Yes," I said bluntly. "You were standing near a floating dead guy, and you had a bag of cash."

Her tone was angry. "I wish you hadn't done that, Lily."

"And I wish I could've spent the evening playing cornball games and exchanging baby presents, but sometimes we don't get what we want."

Tess shuffled anxiously. She raised her thumb to her mouth and bit at the corner. "I've got to go."

"Why did you call me?" I pressed. "You obviously wanted my help."

"I like you, Lily. I...I wanted you to know I didn't do what I'm being accused of."

"But you can't tell me what you were really doing?"

She shook her head and rubbed her hand through her short, layered hair. "It's too dangerous."

Why did everyone think I was helpless? I'd managed shifter dynamics for years. It would have to get hairier than this to scare me off. Pun intended. I shoved on my magic hard and tried again. "Why were you by the pool? What was in the bag? If you didn't kill Wells, did you see who did?"

Her face turned red, and her cheeks puffed out as

she held her breath momentarily and then let it out. She shook her head. "I can't."

"Did you see someone kill Wells?"

After a brief hesitation, she answered, "No."

Ping. First lie.

She started moving toward the door.

I held up my hand to stop her. "Did you know Wells outside of the class?"

"Yes." She put her hand over her mouth. "Forget I came here, Lily. You can't help me."

It was my turn to get angry. "Because you think I'm an idiot who can't see through all your lies?"

Tess shook her head. "Because you're too smart. And smart in my business will get you hurt."

She raced past me, and I moved out of the way. No sense in getting physical when there was a perfectly good deputy on the other side of the door.

When Tess opened the door, I heard Pearl say, "Land sakes, you three, what are you doing hiding in the hall? Darn near gave me a coronary."

Tess jumped into action at the warning and zipped to the right, jumping out of Nadine's reach. Pearl had blocked Buzz so that he couldn't grab her either. Reggie ran after her, but her heel caught on a split in the tile floor, and she threw herself against a wall to keep from falling down. Tess was out the back door. By the time I arrived, she'd started the Suburban, thrown it into reverse, and gunned it.

A loud screech of metal on metal made me scream in horror. "Nooooooooo!"

Nadine, Reggie, Buzz, and Pearl nearly ran me over when they rushed through the door.

"What happened?" Nadine asked.

Reggie had a hand on my back and one on my belly. "Is it the baby?"

"One of my babies," I cried. I inclined my head toward Martha. My mini truck had a dent that extended from the passenger quarter panel to the door and ended at the bed. "Oh, Martha. What has she done to you?"

Nadine was on the phone. "This is Deputy Nadine Booth. I'm at The Cat's Meow on Sterling Street. Yes, good," she said. "You know the place. I need a patrol car over here now. And I need an APB out on a white full-sized suburban with a torn-up bumper." She nodded a couple of times, then said, "Tess Danvers. She's a person of interest in the Wells Neeley case. Just an FYI. She's pregnant. Okay. Thanks."

I stared at my car with a sorrow I couldn't even begin to explain. "What am I going to do now?"

Buzz, who had also been on the phone, told me, "I've called Parker. He's on his way to pick you up."

"Et tu, Buzz?"

His lips flattened in a grim line. "I'm not stabbing you, Lily."

"Just tattling to my mate." I hoped Parker wouldn't be too upset with me for meeting a murder suspect alone. I jerked my chin to Nadine. "She didn't do it," I told her. "She's got secrets, no doubt, but shooting Wells Neeley in the head isn't one of them."

"Are you sure?" Nadine studied my face as she waited for a reply.

I could hear sirens in the distance. "I'm sure. Tess is innocent."

At least of murder.

CHAPTER

TEN

I'd never felt so grumpy in my whole life, which was entirely an exaggeration, but whatever. Sure, a man had died. That wasn't good. But people die. I liked Tess. I'd even wanted to defend her against the accusations she faced, but it was taking every fiber of my good will and generosity not to wish her a long and miserable life behind bars. Only, not for murder, but for truckicide.

Did Martha still start? Yes.

Did Martha drive? No.

The crushed quarter panel had been shoved into the wheel. There was no way to get it down the road on its own. Instead, Parker had called his dad, and Greer had come over with a tow bar and hauled it to his shop.

I noted Parker's white-knuckled grip on the steering wheel as we drove to the shelter to meet Gail and Andi. When he'd shown up at the diner, he'd hugged me firmly, but I could feel his anger and tension vibrating through his body.

"I'm sorry," I said, trying to sound sincere. Not because I wasn't being genuine but because I was so enraged about my truck that it was hard to make an apology sound anything but begrudging.

"You could've been hurt. Our daughter could've been hurt. I'm trying hard not to be unfair to you right now because I'm so afraid I'll say something I won't be able to take back."

I understood why he was scared. He loved me, and I was pregnant with our baby. I loved him more than I could say. Even so, I wouldn't be a prisoner in my body because my actions might worry him. I worried about him all the time. As a pit bull rescuer, there were many times Parker had gone into a sketchy and dangerous situation to save a dog. He'd been chased and threatened, and once, a guy took a shot at him. My heart had nearly stopped beating in my chest when I'd heard about it. Still, I didn't tell him to stop or that he couldn't go do the thing he loved. It was his purpose. And, while I wasn't sure investigating was my *purpose*, it was something I loved.

"What can I do?"

"Can you promise to keep out of harm's way?" he asked, then shook his head. "Again, not fair, but I can't stop the churning dread in the pit of my stomach." He reached over and put his hand on my knee. "I'll move past it," he said. "Just got to feel my feels. Until then, as my mom used to say, if you can't say anything nice, it's okay not to say anything at all."

I laid my hand over his. "Your mom was a wise woman."

He nodded. "Yes, she was."

Part of his purpose had been building the new rescue facility outside of town on a large enough compound to give our shelter dogs the best life they could have without being in a foster or forever home. Parker had taken pride in the fact that he'd had a hand in all the construction, from the pouring of the foundation to the shingling of the roof. As we turned into Pibble Drive, a fun name we'd given to the road leading to the shelter, I felt an enormous swell of pride for my man.

"You never gave up," I told him. "You never do."

He turned his palm up and squeezed my hand. "I couldn't have done it without you."

A few years back, I had found some stolen cash on my property. The reward had been one hundred and fifty thousand dollars. I had done an even fifty-fifty split with Parker so that he could get his dream off the ground. Seventy-five thousand dollars each. I'd used the money to pay off my house. Parker had used his half to pay for the massive amount of concrete needed for the foundation and to get the entire structure roughed in and roofed. Those had been the most expensive items. The rest of the place came together because of generous donors who contributed time, materials, and money.

Theresa Porter, now married to another volunteer of ours, Keith Porter, had been one of those people.

When her husband Jock had died, she'd been in the middle of leaving him. As a result, she'd inherited all of his property, retirement account, and other assets. In other words, it had been a lot of money. She'd donated some of it to an abused women's shelter because she'd lived through years of abuse at her husband's hands, and she wanted to help other women who were dealing with the same terrifying existence. After that, she'd donated a lion's share of Jock's money to the rescue. It had been enough to fund us without too many financial worries for a couple of years.

Several cars were parked out front, along with Keith's old half-ton. Keith and Theresa had an adorable son, Carson, who was over two years old. I was blown away by how fast time flew by. Soon, my girl would be with us. It wouldn't take long for her to go off to school, then college, and maybe, after, travel the world.

I'd said something to that effect to Parker last week. He'd told me to keep dreaming big for her so that she would know she could dream big for herself. It made me love him even more.

I pointed at the blue sedan I didn't recognize. "That must be Gail and Andi's car."

"We're fixin' to find out." He parked in the space on the right next to Keith's truck.

My stomach fluttered, and I wasn't sure if it was the baby or my excitement. One of our long-term furkids was going to get fostered. That meant more socialization, attention, love, and a better chance of adoption.

Parker got out and walked around to my side of the truck. I let him open the door and help me out. He needed to feel like he had some control, even if it was an illusion. I'd seen it with other shifter mates, and the drive to protect went both ways. Allowing him to help me from the truck, even though I was fully capable, would make him feel better, and it cost me nothing to let him.

"Hey," I said softly as I slipped into his arms. "I'm okay, and Tess didn't shoot Wells."

"You don't know that," he said.

I peered up at him. "You know that I do. She told me with no uncertainty that she didn't kill the man. She was telling me the truth."

He looked as if he wanted to argue momentarily but shook his head. "I can't debate magic with you. If you say she's innocent, I believe you."

"Thank you." I rewarded him with a kiss. "I love you so much, and you've made me the happiest woman."

"Happy wife, happy life," he quipped.

I reached around his backside and squeezed his butt. "I've got several ideas for keeping your wife happy later."

"Oh yeah?" His lip curled as his blue eyes drank me in. "I'm very interested in all of them."

I gave his cheeks, and not the ones on his face, a quick pat. "First, dogs."

He pressed his forehead to mine. "First, dogs."

We headed inside, and *woooweee*, let me tell you,

for anyone who has never been in a dog shelter, even a super-clean one like ours, nothing can quite prepare you for the scent. It was a combination of damp dog, industrial solvents, and the light stench of dog waste that lingers long after it's been cleaned up. I didn't mind it one bit.

Theresa wasn't in the office, so Parker and I headed to the chillax room. The room had two couches, a sound system that pumped out easy-listening tunes at a low volume all day, and a handful of comfort toys. It was a safe environment where we took prospective adopters and fosters to meet the dogs.

Gail and Andi were sitting on the sofa, and Theresa was in a chair, holding Carson on her lap.

"Leeeleee," Carson said after he saw me. I thought the way he said my name was sweet and adorable.

"Hey, Car-car." I grinned. "You helping Momma with the dogs today?"

"Doggos," he said. "I want dogs."

"Impressive," I told him. My gaze met Theresa's. "Full sentences, huh?"

She looked proud as a peacock. "Just started doing it this week. I can't believe it," she chirped. "My baby is turning into a fully developed child."

I nodded. "He's a little smarty-pants, for sure." I turned my attention to the young couple. "Hey, you two. So glad you came out today. After last night, I wasn't sure. I was relieved when Parker told me you had called to say you were coming."

Andi held hands with Gail. She looked like she was on the verge of tears. "After last night, I need a dog more than ever."

"It really shook her up," Gail said. "Shook me up, too."

My brow dipped. Did my lie detector just ping? Interesting.

Theresa got up and put Carson on her hip. "Now that you and Parker are here, I'm going to take this one to a play date he has with his nana this afternoon."

"Nana shop!" Carson exclaimed.

Theresa winced. "My mother has been taking Carson to the toy store every time he goes for a visit. She lets him choose one item within reason, but I swear I have to spend the first couple hours I get him back home de-grandma-tizing the boy." She smiled, so I knew it didn't upset her one bit. "She spoils him."

I touched my chest as a surge of emotions caught me by surprise. "That's wonderful." My mother would never know my child, and while I knew she'd be spoiled by all the people who loved me, the realization hit me hard.

"Aww, Lily." Theresa hugged me, squishing a squirming Carson between us. "Your momma will be watching over and spoiling your baby from heaven."

Shifters had their version of an afterlife that was heaven-like. Weirdly, Theresa's platitude made me feel better. "Thanks."

She let me go and looked at Gail and Andi. "So lovely to meet you both."

"You too," Andi replied.

Parker shook hands with the couple, then gestured toward the door leading to the kennels. "I'm going to go get one of the dogs we discussed," Parker said. "You two relax and hang with Lily."

We had three dogs in mind for the couple. They were looking for older, hard-to-adopt boys, so we picked out Rosco, a seven- to ten-year-old, stocky, blue-and-white pit mix. Rutger, a six-year-old relinquished after his owner passed away, was next. The handsome boy was a white American pit bull terrier named after his previous owner's favorite actor, Rutger Hauer. The third one was Leo, a pit and golden retriever mix named after the Lion since the fur around his head was longer than most pitties.

While we waited, I made small talk that I hoped might lead to more information about the victim. "I know that Gail is a loan officer at the bank," I said to Andi. "What is it that you do for a living?"

A worried expression crossed her face. "I put all that on the paperwork."

"Oh, it's nothing like that," I assured her. "I didn't read your foster folder."

Her pinched features relaxed. "Good." She shook her head. "I just didn't want it to be more bad news."

"More?" I leaned forward.

She glanced at Gail. "It's no big deal. Just some —"

"Stuff at school with Gina," Gail lied. "She's a little older than Gabby and going through a bit of a rebellious phase."

I couldn't call him out on it, so I moved on. "Anyhow, what do you do?"

"I'm a divorce attorney," she said.

"I had no idea," I told her. "That's...unexpected."

She tittered a laugh. "I don't know why."

"My wife's a smart cookie," Gail said. "And a real

shark as a negotiator. She's been getting her way with me for fifteen years."

I loved seeing the care and attention between them when they interacted. It made me feel even better about whichever dog they chose to care for.

Andi had said she'd known Wells for a long time, so I asked, "Do you know who might've wanted to hurt Wells?"

Gail flinched. "I imagine a few people. The man could rub an emotional support animal the wrong way."

I choked on a laugh. "I'm sorry. I don't mean to be cavalier since he's dead, but that was funny."

Gail shook his head as a smile quirked his lips. "The man was a son-of-a-bitch, but he didn't deserve this."

That was a truth. "He had a lot of enemies, then?"

"Yes," Andi said. "Wells has been collecting them since high school. He was a bully then, and he is...*was* still a bully." She clenched her fists. "You should talk to Larissa."

"Larissa?" Had the instructor known Wells better than I thought she did? "Why Larissa?"

"She and Wells—"

Gail put his hand on her arm, and she didn't finish the thought. Dang it!

Before I could pry more, Rosco, escorted by Parker on a Bully leash, swaggered into the room and flopped down in front of Gail and Andi, immediately giving them his belly.

Andi's face lit up. "What a sweet floof!"

Rosco had been with us longer than the other two, so I was glad Parker brought him out first. "Our vet says Rosco is between seven and ten years old. He was found abandoned on the streets, no chip, but he had a collar on, so he'd belonged to someone once. We called all the vets in the surrounding areas and all the shelters and couldn't find anyone who knew who he might belong to. He's housebroken, has a super-sweet disposition, and he's been with us for seven months."

"Aww, poor baby," Andi soothed. "You're a survivor, fella, don't you ever forget that."

Gail scooted forward, and Rosco sat up and put his ginormous head on his lap. "He's a real charmer. I can't believe he hasn't been snatched up."

A smear of thick dog saliva coated Gail's thigh.

I winced. "He's a bit of a drooler. I think he has some boxer in him."

"We all have our crosses to bear, don't we, boy,"

Gail said as he scratched under Rosco's chin. "He's great."

"Do we need to see more?" Andi asked after a few minutes. "I'll feel guilty when I have to reject the other two because I think someone is already in love." She put her hand to one side of her mouth and said conspiratorially, "And it's not just the boy with the fur coat."

I burst into tears. Gah. "I'm so sorry."

Andi was crying now, too. "Stupid hormones."

I laughed as tears fell and agreed, "Stupid hormones."

Parker, who had been quietly watching, grinned at the couple. "I'm ready to move forward with Rosco if you are."

CHAPTER
ELEVEN

Smooshie waddled her way over to me when Parker and I got home. Her swishing tail made it impossible for her to walk a straight line, and I was here for it.

I dropped to squat before my baby girl and wrapped my arms around her. I was rewarded with the top of her skull ramming into my chin.

"Owth." I moved my head to the side. "You made me bite my tongue."

Parker shook his head. Elvis was splayed out on the couch. "Don't get up on my account," he told his pooch.

Sal and Donna met with Sparrow shortly after Gail and Andi had taken Rosco home. Sparrow and Sal hit it off immediately. The couple were coming by the shelter tomorrow afternoon to pick her up and take her home. All in all, it had been a really good day. Minus the mashing of Martha, of course.

Elvis, who was part Great Dane, whacked his long tail against the armrest on one side of the couch while he craned his head back on the other. Two of the cushions were on the floor, and I shot an accusing look at Smooshie. "Did you do that?"

My question made her even more excited. "I didn't ask you what you think. I asked you if you did it."

Parker took his phone off his belt and carried it into the kitchen, where we kept the chargers.

I grabbed mine from my purse and handed it to him as he passed. "Take mine too."

"You have a message," he said.

"I didn't get a notification." I held the phone up to my face, and the screen unlocked. "It's from Nadine. She said to call when I got home. She's coming over with Buzz. They'll bring dinner."

"I'm not mad about that," Parker said. "But tell them to make it dinner for six. I got a text from Dad. He and Reggie are coming over because he wants to talk to you about Martha in person."

My heart sank. "That's never a good sign." Especially if he felt like he needed to bring my bestie as backup. I texted Nadine. *Home. Greer and Reggie heading over, too. Bring more grub.*

She shot me a thumbs up back.

I glanced at Parker, who had his phone open and was ready to text. "Let your dad know he's getting fed."

"Done," he replied. He held his hand out. I handed him the phone and went into the living room. I hated to disturb Elvis' beauty sleep, but I made him get up so I could fix the couch. Afterward, I flopped down and put my feet on the coffee table. My ankles were plumper than usual. I'd ask Reggie if there was something I should be doing to keep that from happening.

Parker joined me on the couch, and I tucked my legs under me and curled against him. Goddess, the scent of the man was amazing. Honey and mint. I slid his T-shirt up and buried my face in his chest, rubbing my cheeks against his fur.

He wrapped me in his arms, and I tilted my head back to invite a kiss. His blue eyes were filled with a myriad of emotions. "You're my life, Lily. You and this baby."

"And you're both mine."

"I get so afraid sometimes," he admitted. "I'm always overwhelmed with these strong emotions, destructive urges, and the need to protect you at any cost. It's doing my head in."

"I'm sorry." I caressed his cheek. "I think it's the mate bond. I've heard it can get rough between shifters, and since you're human, it might be more than what you can handle. I wish I knew how to fix it so you could feel...less."

"I don't." He pressed his nose to mine. "I never want to feel less. Not when it comes to you."

I tilted my head back and felt his breath on my cheek as his lips brushed against my skin. I turned to meet his mouth, excited by the firm feel, the sweet taste, and his scent. It was a perfect storm of sensations that made my pulse race.

He pulled me completely into his lap. "If we hurry, we can get started on your happy wife list before everyone gets here."

"Yes," was my answer. "Yes, please."

Twenty minutes later, I was thoroughly happy multiple times. Greer wasn't the only Knowles who knew some tricks, and as soon as I thought the thought, I cursed Reggie for sharing. I picked my clothes up off the floor and laughed as Parker chased me up the stairs to our room.

"Time for a shower?" I asked hopefully.

Smooshie gave several sharp warning barks that we had guests, dashing any hopes of a replay.

Parker threw a pair of shorts on and pulled on a T-shirt as he vacated the bedroom. I thought about what he said, about the overwhelming feelings he'd been experiencing. Was it because of my pregnancy? I'd had my own battle with emotions lately. I literally cried watching a sunrise three days ago. Any more, it seemed as if everything made me cry—good, bad, or ugly. I made a mental note to call Anita later and ask if mated shifter-shifter couples could experience each other's emotions. Hopefully, some of the intensity would dissipate once the baby was here.

I jumped in the shower for a hot second, long enough to wash off the day and a bit of the last twenty minutes, as well. I loved sex as much as the next person, but I didn't want to advertise. I glanced down at my growing belly and giggled. Too late for that, I supposed.

When I made my way down to the foyer, better known as my narrow staircase, Reggie and Nadine were at the bottom, waiting for me.

Nadine whistled. "You get it, girlfriend."

Reggie waggled her brows. "The proverbial walk of shame."

I coughed, trying not to laugh. "There's zero shame. Zero!" When I strode off the bottom step, I glared at them. "You guys are awful," I said, biting back a grin. "I should shop around for new best friends."

"Why look for cheap knockoffs when we're the real deal?" Reggie winked, and it made her look like she had an eye spasm.

I laughed so hard I thought I might go into early labor. "Don't ever do that again," I choked out. "Your eyelashes looked like they were trying to escape your face."

She waved both hands at me in a shushing motion, then grinned. "The guys are in the kitchen."

"Where are the triplets?" I asked.

"With my folks," Nadine replied. "Mommy needs an adult night out."

The scent of chili, garlic, cilantro and other pungently delicious spices wafted down the hall. I grabbed Nadine's hand. "Did he make barbacoa?"

She nodded enthusiastically. "Just for you. Plus, he made a mess of corn tortillas, brought the left-over chicken tortilla soup from the diner, *and* didn't leave out any of the sides. He's got rice, beans, pico, guac, cheese, sour cream, and some spicy salsa."

"If he keeps this up, I'll end up naming my daughter Buzz."

My friends looped their arms in mine and directed me to the kitchen.

The vibrant colors of chopped cilantro and ripe tomatoes, the earthy aromas of chili spices and roasting meat, and the sizzle of corn tortillas frying in the pan were a feast for the senses. Frankly, I couldn't wait for the last two senses to get their due. Touching and tasting.

"Get in my belly," I said, doing my best Mike Meyers impression, which, on the whole, was terrible.

I got a few groans for my effort and took a bow. Then I noticed some bags that weren't food, along with several gallon-sized cans of paint, sitting in the corner of my room. *I will not cry*, I told myself. *I will not cry*.

Dang it, I was crying!

"Awww, Lils." Nadine's lip jutted into a pout as she put her arm around my shoulder.

"It's going to be okay," Reggie added. "See, we have your back. We know you've been worried about not being ready, but you don't have to because we'll make sure you have everything you need and more." She lifted my hand and patted it. "Which reminds me, we've set your baby shower date for two weeks from Saturday if that works for you."

"A baby shower? You guys..." I was now a veritable fountain.

"You've gone and made her cry harder, Reg," Nadine complained.

The three men handling the food looked like they had taken a class on avoiding eye contact and had all graduated with honors.

"Foods about ready," Buzz said. "Why don't you all set out some plates and get ice in the cups for the lemonade I brought?"

I went over and hugged my uncle and possibly got a little snot on his shirt. "If I didn't already love you, Buzz," I hiccupped, "I think tonight would've sealed the deal."

The people in my life, my family, blood and chosen, made haste in setting up the meal. Soon, we were all sitting down to the Mexican feast Buzz had prepared.

Greer said hesitantly, "Lily."

I shook my head and held up a hand. "Not yet," I told him. I wasn't ready to hear bad news about Martha. I gestured to Nadine with my fork before digging into the shredded beef barbacoa and piling it onto my plate's four freshly cooked tortillas. "Did the police find Tess?"

"Nope," she said. "It's like that woman's a ghost, both here and online. And there's nothing in our databases under the name Tess Danvers. How long did she tell you she'd lived in Moonrise?"

"She told me six months ago via Kansas City, but she'd told someone else in our group that she'd come from Fallon. Then she made it out like both statements were true." I added pico, fresh cilantro, tomatoes, guacamole, pickled jalapenos, and sour cream to my tacos.

Reggie's eyes widened. "You're not going to be able to get those closed."

I chuckled. "That's what forks are for. To pick up whatever falls out."

Nadine asked, "Did you get a sense she was lying about those locations?"

"Kansas City was mostly the truth," I answered. "But Fallon was a lie. I'd focus on KC."

"Good tip." She inclined her head. "Can I take your phone to our tech guy?"

"For what?" I didn't want to give up my phone. I had pictures on there and conversations with my witch friend Hazel that could be misconstrued by someone who didn't know that paranormal folk existed.

"Brad Pinion, our new computer forensic specialist, says he might be able to trace the contact."

"It was an unknown number," I said.

"He says he can get around the privacy part of that, and if the phone is on, he can triangulate it. We're in the wind on this one, Lils, and it's making Bobby look bad."

"Did Bobby say that?"

"No, I'm saying it. He's the best thing that's happened to Moonrise since, well, Buzz and you."

"Are we invisible?" Greer asked Reggie.

"I can see you," she told him. "Can you see me?"

"Maybe we're in our own bubble, and while we can see each other, no one else can see us," Greer said with a chuckle.

"Then we might as well get naked." Reggie winked at him, once again causing the flutter effect.

Parker and I both said, "No!"

Nadine snickered. "Fine," she amended. "Best thing since Buzz, Reggie, Greer, and Lily."

I tucked my chin and pursed my lips. "Why am I last?"

"Whatever!" Nadine circled her fork at me. "Can we have the phone?"

"Use Wells' phone," Parker suggested. "He had that threatening text from an unknown caller."

I chewed a perfect bite of taco, juice dribbling down my chin as I nodded emphatically. "That," I finally said when I could swallow. "Use Wells' phone. Unless the tech guy has already tried. If he can't get a trace on the unknown caller from that fancy phone, I don't know why he thinks he can get it from mine?"

Nadine's brow lowered, and her eyes were slits as she stared at Parker and me. "What phone?"

"The one in the classroom. Jeanine set it down on the table with the gifts." I looked at Parker. "Didn't she?"

He shrugged. "Beats me. I wasn't paying attention to her once we saw the text."

"I'll call Gary Hall. He's running the case, but I sifted through the evidence list, and a cell phone wasn't on it."

"Maybe Jeanine took it with her when we left the room and forgot she had it." I was trying to give Wells' wife the benefit of the doubt, but she would have some explaining to do if she hadn't handed the phone over.

"What about Trevor Peters? He passed us on the stairs when we went back to the class to get our things. He could've taken it. He was also missing from the room when Wells died."

"Peters is alibied out," Nadine said. "He couldn't have done it."

"Okay. Good to know." I shifted my gaze to Reggie. "Anything new with the autopsy?"

"Phone?" Nadine asked again, ignoring the fact that I was avoiding her request. "It could be a game changer, Lily."

"Fine," I grumped. "But I want it back ASAP, and if this Brad dude deletes any of my stuff, I will hunt him down. I'm a prey animal. I'll find him, and I *will* hurt him."

Nadine's eyes went wide. "Noted."

Reggie cleared her throat. "I can't talk to you with brown streaks on your chin."

I picked up a napkin and wiped. "Better?"

"Much." She smiled. "Twenty-two bullets are small, so if Wells had been hit anywhere else, he might've survived."

"Aanhn!" Nadine made a buzzer sound. "I'll take urban myths for two hundred. Twenty-two caliber rifles and handguns are the most accessible guns to own and are used in many lethal shootings."

Reggie rolled her eyes. "Good to know, Officer Lacey. I am a criminal medical examiner, but what do I know?"

I snickered.

"I've always fancied myself more of a Cagney. Sharon Gless was hot."

"Yeah, she was," Buzz agreed. Until he caught Nadine's glare and amended, "But no one has anything on my hot cop." He bussed a smooch at her.

"Oh," I told Nadine. "According to one of the parents, Larissa Merriweather might be involved with Wells somehow. They both grew up with Wells, so I asked a few questions. I was surprised when Larissa's name came up, but I should've suspected it last night when I caught her in a lie. I'd asked her if she'd seen him before we'd started our search. She'd said she hadn't, but she was definitely lying. I didn't get any more from the couple, but it's a jump-off point."

"Nice," Nadine approved. "I don't think they were even looking at her past her initial statement. I'll put Gary on it."

Parker scowled, but he didn't comment.

Reggie returned with, "I wasn't done with the forensics."

Nadine held up her hand. "My bad. Go on, Quincy."

I pivoted my gaze between them. "Are you guys watching eighties reruns without me?"

They ignored me.

"There were traces of methamphetamine powder in his mouth and under his nails," Reggie informed us.

Nadine frowned. "Way to bury the lead, Reg."

Reggie tugged the diamond stud earring in her right ear. "That's all I have so far. I have some tox screens still out, and I can't do much to analyze the damage the bullet did to his brain, but I'm guessing it wasn't enough to instantly kill him. I think he might've drowned after he fell in."

"I thought you said earlier..."

"I did," Reggie admitted. "But when I went back for a closer look, the bullet didn't appear to do enough damage to be the cause of death. There was some water in the stomach and the airway, but that would happen whether he'd gone in alive or dead. I'll only rule out a drowning if I can exclude everything else."

"This is some real appetizing conversation," Buzz noted with a wince. "Eat up so we can get the nursery together."

Greer grunted. "And maybe talk about Martha."

"Later," I told him. "I know it's not good, but let me have tonight."

Greer smiled, and it reminded me so much of Parker. "All right, Lily. You get to have tonight."

I gave a contented sigh. "Thank you. All of you. I don't know what my life would've been had I not found you." I slipped my hand over Parker's knee. "I'm glad I never have to know."

Nadine held up her glass of lemonade. "To Lily."

"To Lily," they all agreed as they raised their glasses and waited for me.

I picked my glass up and added, "To my family. The best ride or dies in the world."

Tess was on the loose. Martha was screwed. Wells was still dead. Even so, I had so much hope that it made me want to cry again.

So I did.

CHAPTER
TWELVE

The glow of the full moon against the star-filled sky sent a warmth through me that I hadn't expected. I searched out all the constellations I knew: Canis Major, also known as the Great Dog, a favorite of mine; Ursa Major, the Great Bear; Leo the Lion; and Virgo the maiden, the sign my daughter would be born under.

"Watcha doing?" Parker asked. He stood with his feet near my head. I reached back and rubbed his calf.

"Enjoying the fruit of our labors," I told him. "It's been a good night."

"Great night," he agreed. He studied the room. "It took us a few weeks to figure out which theme." Parker smiled down at me. "I'm glad you like it."

"Like it? I love it." I ran my hand as far up his leg as I could reach. "Join me under the stars."

He got down on the floor and lay on his back next to me. He tugged me into his arms, and I rested my head on his chest.

The nursery had turned out wonderful. Journey's crib was made from weathered reclaimed wood, and Nadine had dry-brushed it with white nontoxic paint designed for baby cribs. Greer had refinished the rocker he'd built for his wife when she was pregnant with Parker. I loved that I would be rocking our daughter in the same chair.

We'd painted the walls a blackened shade of forest green called Fairy Woods. It resembled a medium shade of sage green but had almost an antique feel about it that I loved. There were shelves in a neutral beige-brown called Driftwood Dreams. My friends had added accents of darkened rose and a light blue-green called Beach Glass. Then, to make everything perfect, Parker, Buzz, and Greer painted the stars and moon on the ceiling with glow-in-the-dark paint.

The room wasn't complete, though. I needed blankets, a changing table, baby clothes, diapers, and creams. Nadine and Reggie opened a link to a baby shower wish list they'd started for me and made me add everything I wanted, big, small, expensive, or affordable, to the list. I balked at the expensive part, but they told me that they would check the most expensive things in the store if I didn't learn to live a little.

I let out a happy sigh and reached as far down as I could, skimming my hand across Parker's package.

"That's right. We have some happy wife stuff to take care of tonight."

He angled his hips toward me so that I would have an easier reach. Which I would've happily continued, but unlucky for Parker, Smooshie came in and plopped down next to me. She positioned her back against my legs, her head by my feet. It was her favorite sleeping position.

"Cockblocker," Parker muttered. Smooshie didn't care one teensy bit.

"Let's take this to the bedroom." I kissed his ear and tugged on the lobe with my teeth.

Parker, for a human, let out an impressive growl.

Before anything else could happen, a well-placed kick by our little soccer champion hit my bladder. "Hurry. Help me up," I said with a sense of urgency. "I'm about to pee my pants."

He bounded to his feet and lifted me to a stand. "Your sexy talk needs work."

"Move," I ordered. "If I lose bladder control in front of you, you might not ever see me as sexy again."

He got out of the way. "Fair enough."

———————

THE NEXT DAY we went down to the local mart and bought a smartphone with a minutes plan so that I wouldn't be without a phone while computer tech Brad did his thing. Then it was time to face the music. Or in this case, Greer Knowles and his diagnosis of Martha. To distract myself, I played a game of suspect and motive. The problem was that there were several suspects, but motives were still iffy.

There was Tess Danvers, who was seen standing over the body, and she ran from the crime scene. Throw in the duffel with money, and the case against her seemed pretty clear. The only problem was that Wells had been shot through the top of his head. He would have had to be below Tess for her to shoot him. Maybe kneeling?

No. Reggie would've mentioned stippling around the wound if the shot had been up close and personal. On top of that, I believed Tess when she told me she hadn't killed him. It didn't mean she was completely innocent. Tess knew something, and she was scared enough to hide.

Next was Pete Reynolds, Wells' employee. He and his wife Jackie had some anger issues when it came to Wells and Jeanine. Pete was out of the room during the right period of time, and he had a motive. I wasn't entirely sure what the motive was...yet.

Interestingly, Andi had said Larissa and Wells had something going on between them. Larissa had been suspiciously absent for a long period of time before Jeanine started telling everyone that Wells was missing. Something else bothered me about Larissa that night, but I couldn't quite put my finger on it.

Then we had Jeanine Neely. She was also out of the room for quite a while. She said she'd been looking for Wells, but maybe her innocent act was just that—an act. Whatever the case, we had four possible suspects who had the opportunity. Finding means and motive would be a whole other kettle of worms.

Trevor hadn't been in the room, but his alibi had been verified by the police. I was curious about where he'd been but put that out of my head for now. I needed to keep my focus on viable suspects.

There was also the missing gun and the missing phone. Finding those would be pivotal to the case. Unfortunately, they were probably at the bottom of the nearest lake already.

Parker reached over and rubbed my shoulder. "You ready for this?" he asked.

"Not even a little." Martha had been there for me through thick and thin. She'd been the only consistent, reliable thing I had in my life from the time my parents died until the time I moved to Moonrise.

I rested my head against the truck window. It was time to give up the dream of living happily ever after with my little beater. The Rusty Wrench on Main Street was open from nine in the morning until five at night, usually with only one employee, Greer. Greer had been running his shop since before Parker was born. He and the garage were staples in the Moonrise community.

Not much had changed since my first day in town. The small white brick building with a garage off to the right side had the bay doors opened when we arrived. Greer, wearing grease-stained coveralls, came out the side door of the garage. He still had a full head of wavy gray hair, thick brows, and light blue, almost colorless eyes. Reggie had been a good influence on him. He had a better haircut, and the glow of his skin made me think he'd been dipping into her face products. But even before he'd started up with my friend, the man hadn't had that many wrinkles. I smiled, thinking about how Parker would look when he got to be his dad's age.

"Come on into the office, you two," Greer said. His voice was raspier than usual.

"Are you coming down with something, Dad?" Parker asked as we followed the older Knowles inside.

"Nah. I think the older I get, the worse my aller-gies get. I woke up with a scratchy throat, is all." He dismissed Parker's concerns. "Reggie ordered me some antihistamine-steroid spray. I'll be fine."

Even though we weren't touching, I could feel Parker relax. Mortality was a hard pill to swallow, but everyone aged. Even shifters and witches, albeit at a much slower rate than humans. Even so, watching your parents get older was a scary prospect. Greer was only in his mid-fifties and had so many more years of life to live. Pearl and Opal Dixon were examples of human beings finding ways to stay young even into their seventies and eighties.

The sign on the office door hadn't changed in

the past five years. It still said: *No Credit Cards. Cash Only. Some Local Checks Accepted (Except from Earl— You Know Why, Earl! You check-bouncing bastard.).* I laughed the first time I read it, and I laughed now.

"When are you going to let Earl off the hook?" I asked Greer.

"Never," he replied. "He still owes me eighty-two dollars and sixty-four cents, twenty-five of which were bank fees for depositing a bounced check."

We followed Greer out the side service exit to where Martha was parked behind the shop. In the bare light of a new day, she looked even worse than when Greer had hauled her off yesterday.

"Oh, Martha." I've never been a pearl clutcher, but if I'd been wearing them, they would've been clutched hard. "Tell me straight, Greer. Just make it quick."

"Insurance isn't going to cover repairs. It's cheaper to total the old girl out than fix the damage."

I'd been expecting the news, but it was still devastating. "How much will insurance pay out on it?"

"Do you want the good news or the bad news?"

"If there's good news, I always want that first."

"Martha's a classic, so she's actually worth more than you might think."

I suddenly had visions of living the highlife on a yacht somewhere off the coast of France. "Life-changing money?"

"Nope." Greer scratched the five o'clock shadow darkening his jawline. "But enough for a healthy down payment on another vehicle. It's a little over five thousand dollars if you want to go ahead and total her out."

For a brief moment, I was stunned to silence.

"Are you joking?"

"I'm not," he said.

"I never thought I'd get more than five hundred for her if I tried to sell her, and all it took to make her worth something was to have her smashed to bits." I chewed the inside of my cheek for a moment.

Greer and Parker watched me warily, unsure of how I'd react. I didn't blame them. I was all over the place mood-wise. But even I was surprised at the emotion that swept through me. I started laughing and laughing. It took several minutes of stops and starts for me to finally stop. Martha had taken care of me during her life and she was still taking care of me in her afterlife. She was and always would be one of my most cherished friends. As I stared at her, overcome with love, I whispered, "I'll miss you old girl...but thank you."

"So, you're not upset?" Parker asked. "Or is laughing the new crying?"

"Maybe a little of both." I flicked my gaze to Greer. "How fast could I get the money?"

"A day or two at the most." Greer shrugged. "It's usually pretty quick."

The decision had been made. It had been made for me, but some things happened for a reason.

"You want to go used-car shopping?" I peered up at Parker. I had an idea that would maybe get more information from the case while providing me with a vehicle solution. "We could go to Moonrise Motors."

He gave me a wary look. "What are you up to?"

I held out my hands as if to say, *are you talking about lil' ol' me?* "I just want to see if they have anything that would be suitable and in our price range."

"And talk to Pete Reynolds about where he was when Wells was killed," Parker guessed.

"If he's around," I said nonchalantly. "You know, just to check in and see how he's holding up."

And to see if he grew tired enough of Wells'

shenanigans to harm him. Jackie had told Pete to end it. Maybe she'd meant permanently.

There was only one way to find out, and it wasn't by sitting around moping about my truck. Martha's demise wouldn't be in vain, I swore. She was going to go out an over five-thousand-dollar hero.

CHAPTER
THIRTEEN

Moonrise Motors was on East Young Street near the edge of town. The lot was full of new vehicles lined up like full-sized Matchbox Cars. Customer parking was to the right, and the show-case storefront was a large blue and silver building with clear glass walls, making it easy to see the fancy new models inside.

Larry Campbell was a tall, athletic-looking man with short brown hair and a spray tan that smelled like soapy coconut. He was also the salesman who had talked to Parker about the thirty thousand dollar mini-SUV. He greeted us like we were long-lost family who had finally been reunited. Ick. The minute he shook my hand, I wanted to wash it.

"Great to see you, Parker," Larry said, clapping my husband on the shoulder. "I knew you'd be back."

"Not for that car," I told the eager man. "It's out of our price range. We need something used, low miles, and that we can get in for less than ten grand." I narrowed my gaze at him. "And when I say less, I don't mean nine-thousand nine hundred and ninety-nine, got me?"

Larry put up his hands in surrender. "Uncle," he said, trying to hide his disappointment. He kind of failed. Not my problem. "I know better than to argue with a woman who knows her mind." He gestured with a flourish toward the lot. "I might have a vehicle that fits the bill. Pun intended." He sounded like a donkey braying as he laughed at his bad joke.

As we followed him past the new cars on the lots, I leaned into Parker and said, "What a jackass. Pun intended."

He chuckled. "Good one."

"Here it is," Larry said, pointing at a green Cadillac SRX. "A beauty of a car. It's twelve years old but only has forty-five thousand miles on it. One owner prior. Clean title." He opened the driver's door. "It has heated leather seats, a sunroof, an aftermarket backup camera and a smart radio. It's sleek, stylish, agile, and one of the smoothest and quietest rides you'll ever drive." He nodded at me. "And since you folks are starting a family, or maybe you already have one, safety locks are in the back so that the doors can't be accidentally opened when the vehicle is in Drive."

My heart raced in my chest as I looked inside the vehicle. It smelled just like the new car scent that Parker liked to hang in his truck.

Larry popped the hatch on the back. "There is a huge amount of storage space in the back." He walked around the side, opened the back driver's side door, and put the seats down.

"That's almost as big as my truck bed now," Parker mused. "There's room for a kennel or two."

He sounded as impressed as I felt. "This is really nice," I said in a throaty whisper. "What's the price?"

Larry put the seats back into their upright position. "If you promise not to hurt me, I'll tell you." He flashed me a smile that was meant to be charming.

I bared my teeth. "Just give me the price, Larry."

"Okay," he said cheerfully. "The lady does not play. The sticker price is eleven thousand two hundred dollars." When I started to protest, he held up a finger. "But for cash, you could drive it off the lot for nine thousand even."

I couldn't stop my body from vibrating with excitement. I tugged on Parker's arm. "Confab. Now."

He nodded, then said to Larry, "Give us a minute."

"Take your time, folks, but this one will sell fast."

I glared at the salesman, and he averted his gaze.

When we were out of hearing distance, Parker said, "You're in love, aren't you?"

I made a face that might've made me look constipated. "Yesssss," I hissed. "How could you tell?"

"I've only seen your face light up twice like that before. The first time you saw Smooshie and the first time you saw me."

I smacked his chest. "Not funny."

"I'm not trying to be funny. Look, I match people with dogs all the time, and I know the look of insta-love. You got it, babe."

"It's sad how much I want that car. And did you see the color? It's green. Like Martha. It's like the old girl is giving me her blessing to move on!"

158

"Okay," Parker said quietly. "Keep it down. We don't want him to know you're already sold."

"Right, right." I smoothed my hair as best I could. Kissed my fingertips and rubbed my belly. Parker raised his brow. "It's for good luck," I said. "It works for Buddha, and I look like Buddha, so..."

"So, let's go get you a vehicle." He curled two fingers at Larry and beckoned him over.

"Did you all make a decision?" the salesman asked.

"Will you take eight grand?" Parker asked. "Cash."

Eight sounded like a whole lot, but I reminded myself I was going to get five of that from insurance.

Larry's forehead wrinkled as he shook his head. "I could knock a couple hundred off and go as low as eighty-eight hundred."

"Eighty-four," Parker countered.

"Eighty-five, and you got yourself a deal."

"Sold," Parker stated. "Let's do it."

"You drive a hard bargain, sir. Let's do it." Larry inclined his head toward the showroom. "Let's go to my office and draw up the paperwork."

As we walked back, I whispered to Parker, "That was stupid hot."

He gave me a lopsided grin. "Goal."

We passed several large garage doors, reminding me why I wanted to come in the first place. "Hey, Larry."

The tall man glanced back. "Did we forget something?"

"I'd like a test drive and to meet your mechanic who certified the vehicle."

I had to hand it to Larry. He didn't even flinch. "I'll get the key for you and see if Pete's in."

FOR STARTERS, for all of Larry's quirks, the spray tan and the laugh, he was excellent at his job. In a few minutes, he handed me the key and told me that Pete would meet me out by the vehicle.

I told Parker he could stay and fill out the paperwork, but he wasn't having it. For some reason, he didn't want me hanging out alone with a murder suspect. Go figure.

Pete Reynolds stood by the bumper of the green beauty. When he saw us, he looked surprised and then confused. "Lily and Parker. What are you all doing here?"

"Buying a car," I said. "We'd love for you to go along on the test drive so we can pick your brain."

"About the SRX?" he asked.

I gave him my best feral smile. "Sure."

Parker opened the back passenger door. "Get in," he ordered in a tone that didn't leave room for an argument.

When Pete slid into the vehicle, Parker closed the door, walked around the car to the driver's side and got in the back next to Pete.

I had the keys, so I got into the driver's seat. I sat for a moment, enjoying the way the ergonomic seats cupped my derriere. The key was a fob. I pointed it at the dash and clicked it. Nothing happened. "How do I start this thing?"

"Just push the button to the right of the steering wheel," Pete said. "As long as you have the fob with you and your foot on the brake, it will start right up."

And oooooh, my gosh, did it start! The engine purred like a cougar shifter on catnip. "All right," I said eagerly. "Let's get this party started."

I backed out of the parking space and headed to the exit. I couldn't believe how quiet the vehicle was or how smooth it traveled over the parking lot. Larry had not exaggerated. This was a cloud on wheels. Once I exited the lot and pulled out onto Young

Street, I glanced back at Pete in my rearview mirror and asked, "Why did you kill Wells?"

Pete's hand went to the door handle as if he planned to make a break for it.

"Child locks," I told him. "Those doors aren't opening until we park this sucker. So you might as well answer the question."

"Are you wearing a wire? Is this a police setup? I won't go down for something I didn't do. You're not going to trick me again," he rambled.

Again? "Why do you think we're wired up?"

"The policeman who talked to me. He warned me to keep my mouth shut about—" Pete shook his head. "No, I can't. I'll lose everything."

"What are you talking about, Pete? Just tell me the truth," I demanded. "Did you kill Wells?"

"Stop asking me that!" he cried. He put his palms against his temples. "Stop it. Just stop."

Parker crossed his arms over his chest and stared at the scared man. "Answer the question?"

"They'll hurt me. They'll hurt Jackie. I can't. I just can't." Pete was having a complete breakdown. "I have a baby on the way. I didn't want any of this. It's all Wells' fault, he made me do it."

"He made you kill him?" I needed clarification.

He'd said he hadn't done it earlier, and I believed him, but I also believed him now. "Or was it something else?"

"No, no, no. Arrest me or let me go," he pleaded. "I'm a little fish in a network of sharks. If they find out we've talked..."

"They won't find out," I promised. The man looked ready to break out a window and jump out. "Just calm down."

"What did Wells make you do?" Parker asked. "We want to help you."

Pete wanted to talk. Badly. I felt it with all of my senses. We needed him to talk, so I gave him a little magical mental push. If he'd killed Wells, I was taking this test drive to the sheriff's office. If he hadn't, he clearly had a darn good idea who did.

"He was blackmailing me." Pete's whole body shook. "That's how they get their claws into you. It was one mistake. One terrible night, and I'll pay for it for the rest of my life."

"Is that what Jackie wanted you to break off? Did she find out about the blackmail and tell you to figure out how to end it?"

Pete sobbed, "She thought it was something else. I couldn't tell her the truth. I think she..."

Parker's voice was low. "You think she what?"

When Pete didn't answer, I concentrated my mojo again and asked, "What do you think Jackie did?"

"I think she killed Wells." Tears and snot were flowing now. "She killed him to save me."

CHAPTER

FOURTEEN

As soon as we got back to the dealership, Pete scrambled out of the vehicle. I pivoted in the seat to talk to Parker. "This car is the best thing I've ever driven."

"You've driven my truck," he said.

"Exactly!" I met his gaze. "I need to call Nadine about Jackie, right? If Jackie managed to murder Wells, then the timeline is definitely skewed. I'll call Reggie after." We got out, and I handed him the fob. "Go talk to Larry. See you in a bit."

Parker headed for the storefront, and I got my phone out.

"Lily? Is that you?" Jeanine tottered across the parking lot toward me. With two babies on board, she was easily twice my size, poor thing. "What are you doing here?"

"Buying a car." I smiled sympathetically. "How are you holding up?"

"Awful," she said. "They won't release Wells' body, so I can't plan his funeral. My kids don't understand why Daddy isn't coming home, and I don't know how to do this alone."

I held my finger up. "Just a minute." I texted Nadine. *Pick up Jackie Reynolds. Her husband thinks she killed Neeley to save him.*

You think she did it?

Maybe. Who knows?

Talk soon.

I focused back on Jeanine. "Sorry. It was a matter of urgency." I left off the part where I was worried her cousin murdered her husband.

"I understand. It's the same for me. I want to be home for my children and console them, but Wells left behind so much that has to be sorted."

"Anything I can help with?" The offer sincere, but there was also a double motive. Helping meant more access to Wells and the possible reasons for his death.

"I've got it handled, but thank you." She peered

past me. "Is that the car you're getting? The Cadillac?"

"Yes," I told her. "I'm really excited for it."

"That one shouldn't have gone up for sale." Jeanine looked worried.

"Is there something wrong with it?" Her statement made me anxious. I didn't want anything coming between me and my new-to-me car.

"Nothing like that." She shook her head and shrugged. "Larry's in charge now. If he doesn't think it needs to go to auction, then I'm sure it's fine. It's just that Wells usually took trade-in cars to the dealer auction that happens over in Centerville once a month. He never sold them on our lot." Her frown wrinkled her brow. "Oh, well. I'm sure it's fine. I never understood why he did it in the first place. They buy and sell vehicles at rock-bottom prices at those things. Of course, Wells sold more than he bought." She dabbed at her eye with a crumpled piece of tissue. "Congratulations. I hope your car lasts you for many, many years."

"Thank you, Jeanine." I reached out and took her hand. "If you need anything, even if it's just an ear. You call me, okay?"

She gave me a startled look and then nodded. "Thank you, Lily. I don't have a lot of people offering support right now. I loved Wells, and he was good to me, but he was a jerk to a lot of people. Not everyone is sorry he's dead."

Like her cousin, for instance.

"Oh, before I go, did you take Wells' phone from the room the other night? The police don't have it."

"No. I set it down on the table by the presents."

At least my memory wasn't slipping. "That's what I thought."

Jeanine hadn't set off my truth-mojo once. Everything she'd told me had been the truth. Had it been helpful? Maybe, maybe not. But one thing I felt more certain about was that the woman hadn't been involved in her husband's murder.

"Do you know of anyone who would want him dead?" I asked.

Her dark blue eyes widened. "Oh, yes," she said emphatically. "Like I told the police. Lots of people wanted him gone. He had more enemies than friends." Her gaze was stark. "I'm worried the only people who will show up for his funeral are the ones who want to double-check he's not coming back."

Parker finished the paperwork, then came and got me. We had to run to the bank and get the money, but after, *Celine* would be mine. No, not Celine. *Lullabelle*? Maybe. Whatever I named her, it would be for her life. Like Martha, I planned to keep *Jujubee* for as long as she lasted.

The bank was only a few blocks from the dealership, so it would be a quick in, get the cash, and out. We had a little over fifteen thousand in our joint savings account. I felt uneasy about taking eight thousand eight hundred and fifty-three dollars out of the account. It had taken a lot of scrimping to save that much. But I was sure about *Sweet Susie*, as sure as I had been about Smooshie, so that was saying a lot. *Andromeda* was mine. I could feel her in my bones. Okay, maybe not the same as Smoosh, but Parker had been right. It had been love at first sight for me and *Penny*. No, that wasn't quite right either.

"I can't pick a name," I said when Parker turned into the bank parking lot. "Nothing sounds right."

"We have time to worry about that. She's not coming for a few months, and when she arrives, I'm sure we'll know exactly what to call her."

I gave him an exaggerated grimace. "I was talking about the SRX."

He rolled his eyes and laughed. "Of course, you were." He turned the truck off. "What about *Gladys*?"

I mulled it over for a moment then grinned. "Maybe. Gladys isn't a bad name—not bad at all. I knew a Gladys when I was growing up. She was a mongoose shifter who had been kind to me when I needed it the most. She used to call me her little shifter sister."

"Sounds like a winner." He got out and walked around to my side of the truck, opened the door and helped me down. "I think you and Gladys are going to have a long beautiful friendship."

"*Charlotte*," I said. "What do you think of that name?"

"If you like it, I like it." He got distracted by something across the street.

"What?" I asked as I tracked his gaze. At the gas station on the other side of the intersection, Larissa Merriweather was pumping gas.

"That's our teacher, right?"

"Yes," I said.

"Small world."

"Agreed," I told Parker as we strolled up the sidewalk to the lobby doors. "Even smaller, she's putting gas in the silver sports car from the day Wells nearly got his butt beat at the park."

"Oh, right. Someone in a silver sports car picked up the guy with the stocking cap."

"I think the someone has been revealed." I took my phone from my purse to text Nadine again. I had several missed messages. Including one that read: *Thanks for the tip. Found .22 rifle.*

Confession?

Not yet. Still enough for an arrest. Talk tonight.

Result, I typed back. *Congrats.* Then added, *Silver car from park at gas station across from bank. Driver Larissa Merriweather.*

Nadine sent back a shocked-faced emoji followed by a clown face.

Since they'd already made an arrest, Nadine might not feel the need to take the silver car thing any further. Was that the end of it? Had the murderer been caught? Possibly, but I couldn't shake the feeling that this case was far from over. I took Parker's hand. "They arrested Jackie."

"Did they find something?"

"Could be. They found a twenty-two." I knew that until a ballistics test, there was no way of telling if it was the right gun. "Lots of people own twenty-twos."

Parker opened the door for me, and I was hit with a wave of airconditioned air. "Even us," he said. "I got my dad's old twenty-two pistol in the fire safe."

"Let's get the money and go." My conversation with Jeanine had unsettled me. It felt like the Charlie Brown-Lucy football scenario. All Charlie Brown wants is to punt the ball, but Lucy keeps yanking it out from under him. All I wanted at this moment was *Audrey*, and Jeanine's talk about how she wasn't supposed to be for sale, made me feel as if she were holding the football, ready to yank it away.

As Parker filled out the withdrawal slip, Gail waved at us from his office. I smiled and waved back. "You got this?" I asked Parker. "I want to say hi to him."

"And check up on Rosco," he added.

"Definitely." Baby girl Knowles moved around, letting me know that she was with me and doing her thing. I rubbed the aching muscles that ran alongside my stomach. "I feel you, girl."

Gail was grinning hard when I made my way over. "Jimin is the absolute best. Andi and I can't thank you and Parker enough for all you do. It took about two seconds for him to feel at home."

"Jimin?"

"Oh, yeah, that." He gave a slight head shake and eye roll combo. "Gina and Gabby are fans of K-pop music, and their favorite band is BTS, and Jimin is their favorite singer from the group. So, poor Rosco is no longer Rosco. He's Jimin. Strange enough, the name suits him, and he is completely delighted every time the girls call him by his new name."

My grin split my face. "Sounds like he's in completely capable hands." I glanced over to Parker. He was at the teller's window. "I better get back. I'm getting a new car today. A mini-SUV."

"Exciting," Gail said. "Congratulations."

"Thank you," I replied. "And congratulations to you too."

He frowned. "For what?"

"Oh, for whatever." The man had to know that he was the proud parent of a dog name Jimin, but until he officially declared the love-a-bull pupper his own, I'd keep the information to myself.

We got the money, and I was more nervous than a cat in a room full of rocking chairs. As we exited the bank, Trevor brushed passed us.

"Hey," I said when he almost knocked me down. The scent of his cologne was enough to make me gag. He squinted at me as if he hardly saw me, then hurried inside. "What a dick."

"Agreed." Parker put his arm around me. "Let's go get your Charlotte."

"Madison." I snapped my fingers. "Or maybe Wendy."

"I hope we don't have this kind of trouble naming our daughter. Baby Jane Doe won't fly on a college application."

"Sweet Jane! It was my favorite song when I was a teenager. I couldn't get enough of Cowboy Junkies. I played the tune so much my mom threatened to break my record." I threw myself into his arms and kissed him. "It's perfect."

Parker eyed me warily. "We're not naming our kid Sweet Jane."

I laughed. "The car, dear." I wagged my chin at him. "The SRX is officially my Sweet Jane."

CHAPTER

FIFTEEN

L ess than two hours later, I was driving Sweet Jane over to Greer's to have him give her an inspection. Parker followed me over. Greer said he'd work it in later this afternoon. Yay. He told me he'd keep her overnight, and I could pick her up in the morning. If all went well, my new girl would be licensed, registered, and ready for me to drive by tomorrow.

"What do you want to do now?" Parker asked after we dropped off Sweet Jane and we were back on the road.

"I need to run," I told him. "Can we go home? I need to feel the fur on my skin and the wind on my face."

He rubbed his arm. "You sure?"

"Positive. I changed into my cougar form every month of this pregnancy, and it's been fine. I can't keep living scared. I'm tired of always waiting for the other shoe to drop, so I'm throwing away all the shoes."

Parker chuckled. "I see you're feeling better about Martha."

"I'm feeling better about everything," I replied. "I want to be happy." I rested my hand on his thigh and leaned my head against his shoulder. "Let's be happy."

"That sounds like a good plan." He turned and kissed my forehead. "I've been happy for a while, so pardon me if I have a head start."

I gave him a sly smile. "Me too, but it's hard to put away old fears. The ones that tell you that the people you love leave and that your dreams are always out of reach."

"Aw, babe. Your parents didn't leave you, and neither did Danny. They were taken from you, and it's understandable that the loss you've experienced can make you feel as if you were abandoned. I've been there."

"Your mom," I said softly. "You lost her too soon. How did you get past that feeling?"

"A combination of therapy and you." He turned

off the highway and onto our road. "You're the best medicine."

"I feel the same way." I tilted my head back, squinting as the sun hit my eyes. "You know, you missed your second calling."

"What's that?"

"You would've made a wonderful therapist. The way you are with dogs, you're the same with people. You know how to say and do the right thing, even when the right thing is doing nothing."

"I think you're giving me a lot of credit where it isn't due." He lifted his arm and dropped it over my shoulders. "I am who I am because you came into my life. You save me."

"You saved me," I said. We'd had this conversation before, and it wasn't any less true now than it was then. "Even so, you've become quite the Zen master."

He chuckled. "I'm glad it looks like that from the outside."

We arrived home, and the first thing I did was get naked and head out the back door where my ten wooded acres awaited. I was ready to go wall-to-wall fur with my running mates. Unfortunately, they were more interested in chasing off critters.

Smooshie and Elvis were barking like crazy at something rustling in the woods.

"How many times do I have to tell you both that squirrels are not the enemy?"

One of my best friends was a squirrel. Well, a familiar in the form of a squirrel. The first time she'd met Smooshie, my pup had chased Tizzy up a tree. To this day, the squirrel hasn't forgiven my girl. Every time I talked to Hazel on the phone, Tizzy made a comment to the effect. I missed both Hazel and Tizzy, but I didn't miss Paradise Falls.

Smooshie took off at a run, charging the trees. "Smoosh!" I shouted. "Come back!"

Parker was on the back steps laughing. "You look like a pregnant tree nymph."

"You wouldn't say that if you'd actually ever met one." His stunned expression made me laugh back.

I heard a scream, then a woman shouting, "Get away! Stay back!"

Well, shoot. So much for a furred-out run. Instead, I was a naked pregnant woman, high-stepping it through the dense brush to keep my dog from hurting someone or getting hurt. "This is private property," I hollered. "Smooshie! Smooshie, don't eat her!"

Smooshie had never attacked anyone in all the

time she'd been with me, so I really doubted there would be any bloodshed, but any animal or person could become dangerous if provoked.

By the time I found her, she was jumping around the base of the tree, her ears perked and tail wagging as if she'd caught a unicorn. And in a way, she had. Five feet up on the lowest branch of one of the oak trees, Tess Danvers was perched and hanging on for dear life. There was something that looked like a round pillow made of something jiggly on the ground. Parker showed up, out of breath, a few seconds later.

"What the hell is going on?"

"Tess," I pointed to the scared woman. "Smooshie treed herself Moonrise's most wanted."

"And this?" He grabbed the jiggling mass from the ground before Smooshie could treat it like a chew toy. "It looks like a—"

"It's a fake pregnancy belly." I was numb with disbelief. No wonder everything Tess said had felt like a lie. "You're not pregnant."

Tess shook her head. "I'm not pregnant."

"Why are you here?" I demanded. Smooshie, now that she'd finished her part of the job and no one was trying to kill anyone, flopped onto her back and began to rub herself Snoopy-style in the grass.

Tess visibly relaxed. "I'm sorry, Lily. You're the first person in this town that I felt like I could trust."

My lips thinned. "Too bad the feeling isn't mutual."

"Why are you naked?" she asked.

"This is my land. I'm allowed to run around naked if I want. You, on the other hand, are a wanted fugitive, and you're trespassing on private property. Your list of felonies continues to grow. Now, you have one minute to convince me not to whoop your butt and turn you in."

Tess' surprise delighted me. People underestimated me all the time, and they were fools because of it. I might be small, but I am mighty.

"My name isn't really Tess Danvers."

"Well, duh." Nadine's search for Tess in the police database had come back with no hits or matches. "Keep talking. Starting with your real name."

"Theresa Davenport, though I've gone by Tess, my nickname, for years. Not everything I told you was a lie. I was pregnant before, and my husband did die. When he did, the stress of it caused me to miscarry."

She was telling the truth, and while I felt tremendously sorry for her, this information wasn't an explanation as to why she was in Moonrise posing as a pregnant woman.

"Why did you come to Moonrise?"

"To find the man who killed my husband." Her blunt words resonated with resounding truth. "I'm a DEA agent, and so was my husband, Carlos. He worked in special investigations and drug trafficking in the undercover division. He hadn't been undercover in years but worked as a handler for several agents."

She took a deep breath. "He discovered one of his agents had gone in too deep and was taking a cut of the drug pie. On top of that, the agent was setting up raids against competitors of the group he worked with. He'd told me that much but never told me who the undercover agent was. Carlos was executed." Her voice choked. "I traced the undercover agent to Moonrise, but I haven't been able to discover his identity. I knew from Carlos' notes that Wells Neeley was involved, so when I found out his wife was pregnant and taking the birthing class, it looked like an opportunity to get more information without outing myself."

"In all the time you've been here, you haven't discovered who the agent is?" Parker asked. "Is it a woman or a man?"

"I think a man. Carlos was always careful to use the word agent and gender-neutral pronouns. It's how they're taught so they can keep their agents safe."

"What were you doing in the pool area?" I asked.

A blustery noise of exasperation escaped her. "I saw Wells go inside. I waited a few minutes, then followed him in. There was a pop sound, like an air gun, from somewhere up high. Wells dropped into the water. There was blood coming out of his head, and that's when I realized he'd been shot, and the pop of air was because a silencer had been used."

Everything she was saying matched up with the forensics. "And the duffel?"

"It was full of cash and drugs," she said. "I took it for leverage."

"Against who?"

"Whoever killed Carlos!" She flung her hands in the air, then instantly realized her mistake as she helicoptered her arms to regain her balance. No joy. Tess dropped like a sack of potatoes, landing hard on the ground. She groaned as she rolled over. Smooshie got up and trotted over to the downed woman and began to unceremoniously lick her face.

Tess rolled to her side. "Oh Lord, make it stop!"

"Smoosh," I said firmly. "Enough." She ignored

me. I didn't bother to hide my smirk. Ah, well. I tried.

Parker waited patiently to see if I had any more questions before he spoke. "Is she telling the truth?"

I nodded. "She is."

"Okay then. I'll meet you back at the house." He tucked the pregnancy belly under his arm then cuffed my loveable derp on the ear to get her attention. "Come on, Smoosh. You've had your fun, and it's time to go."

I helped Tess from the ground. "Coffee?"

"Yes, please."

"Follow me."

She kept averting her gaze whenever her eyes settled in my direction. "You'll be putting some clothes on, right?"

"Does my nakedness on my very private property bother you?" I asked.

"I take your point."

As we got closer to the house, I heard someone talking to Parker inside our home. I motioned for Tess to hold her position as I ran up the steps, careful to stay quiet, and peeked inside. Nadine was sitting in the kitchen.

I waved Tess over. "It's just my friend Nadine."

"The cop?"

I nodded. "The cop."

When Tess tried to bolt, I grabbed her arm and kept a firm grip. She looked like she was about to slug me when I gestured to my protruding tummy. "You really want to hit a naked pregnant woman?"

I tapped on the window with my free hand. "We're coming in," I said loudly. To Tess, I added, "Go inside, and don't do anything stupid, okay?"

"Fine," she said. "But I've gotten pretty good at stupid lately, so I can't make any guarantees."

CHAPTER
SIXTEEN

Parker had called Nadine before chasing after me into the woods. She'd arrived when Tess was up the tree. I went upstairs and put on clothes, much to Tess' relief. *Sheesh. Humans.*

By the time I got back down to the kitchen, Nadine looked ready to spit nails.

"You're telling me a drug traffic ring is working out of Moonrise?" She scoffed. "Impossible. The counties surrounding is where all the meth is landing."

Parker had made a pot of coffee, and there was iced tea in the fridge. I poured a cup of java for Tess and a tall glass of tea for Nadine before sitting down at the table with them.

"Reggie did say that Wells had traces of meth inside his mouth and under his fingernails."

Nadine stammered, "Yeah, but—"

"Yeah, but," Tess said, "the DEA has its eyes on several operations where the drugs are being manufactured in one county and then dispersed to the surrounding areas. These rings don't sell drugs where they make them. It's why they're so difficult to track. They're smart, too. There are no street transactions. Carlos couldn't figure out how they were transporting or selling the drugs, and his agent had drunk the Kool-Aid."

"I'm going to have to verify your story," Nadine told her. "Is there anyone I can call with the DEA who can vouch for you?"

Tess shrugged. "I was put on mandatory leave when I tried to break into Carlos' files and figure out who the undercover agent was. They keep things on a need to know, and I couldn't get anyone to believe me about who killed my husband. As far as the agency is concerned, Carlos' man in the field is producing results. There are busts being made all over southern Missouri because of this guy, but it's all smoke and mirrors to keep the law from the real power behind the curtain."

Nadine put her elbows on the table. "And you think it was Wells Neeley?"

"I still do," Tess confided. "But I think someone made a power play to take his spot. I think it's the agent, but it's a guess. I don't have any hard evidence."

Something Jeanine had said to me earlier tickled at the back of my mind. "Could it be possible that the drugs are being transported by trade-in vehicles and being sold at dealer auctions? Jeanine said that it was weird that Larry was selling me my new car. She said Wells never kept the trade-ins. He always took them to auction."

Tess stared at me as if I'd grown a third eye.

"What?" I asked.

"That's such a deviously simple plan and completely doable. Take a trade-in, stuff it with drugs, and sell it at an inflated price at auction. The dealers take the drugs, the dealerships sell the cars at a loss, and get to write it off on their taxes as the cost of doing business." She blinked at me. "That's freaking brilliant."

Nadine nodded. "Lily's a bright bulb in a world of candles. But how do we prove it?"

"Oh, no," I moaned.

"That's never a good sign," Parker, who'd been listening quietly, said. "What are you thinking?"

"I'm thinking that if Larry wasn't supposed to sell the car because it was going to auction, then maybe—"

"The car is loaded with drugs!" Nadine said brightly.

"Don't sound so excited," I told her. "Whoever is trafficking those drugs is going to want them back, and my Sweet Jane is currently at The Rusty Wrench."

Parker grabbed his keys and phone from the counter. "Let's go."

Tess rode in the back of the truck, and Nadine followed us in her car. She'd wanted to take the lead, but Parker wasn't about to wait if his father was in danger. The worst part, I'd been calling Greer over and over, and he had yet to pick up. *Dear Universe,* I thought, *Don't let anything happen to Greer.*

I couldn't believe I'd let my guard down. Of course, the minute you start thinking the world is a good place, the world slaps the notion right out of you.

We broke several speeding laws and got into town faster than usual. I tried not to panic. Greer could be under a car for all we knew and hadn't heard his phone. Even still, I couldn't stop all the awful scenarios from playing out in my head.

When we got to The Rusty Wrench, the bay door was locked, and so was the office. I pressed my face to the window.

"See anything?" Parker asked.

"No," I told him. "No one is in the office."

Nadine had her phone out. "Hey, Reggie. Is Greer at home?"

I dialed in my ears and heard Reggie say, "No, he's working late tonight. He had some specialty foreign car that he'd been waiting on parts for, and he wanted to make sure to get Lily's SUV inspected. I know he planned to be thorough because he wanted to make sure she had a safe vehicle."

My stomach clenched. If Greer was in trouble because of me, I was going to hurt someone.

Reggie's tone changed as if she suspected there was more. "What's going on? Greer's okay, isn't he?"

The three of us didn't lie to each other. Nadine, as gently as she could, told her, "We're at his shop now, and we can't find him. We think he might've gotten caught up with something dangerous because of Lily's car."

"That makes no sense," she said as the panic in her voice rose.

"We think there might be drugs in the car." Nadine squeezed her eyes shut for a second. "I have to go."

"Find him," Reggie demanded.

"We will," Nadine promised. "Try to call him and keep calling. This could all be a big misunderstanding."

It was a nice thought, but none of us believed it.

"When does that Centerville dealers auction take place?" Jeanine had said it was once a month, but she didn't say when.

Parker searched for it on his phone. "It's tonight," he said. "At seven o'clock."

"That's just a little over six hours from now. Would they take Greer with them?" I asked Tess.

"He's a witness," Tess said flatly. "We should get to Centerville as quickly as possible."

"I have a few friends at the sheriff's department in Remir County. Centerville is the county seat. I'll call them and have them keep an eye out for the vehicle." She looked at me. "Give me the make, model, and color."

"Cadillac SRX, dark green. It has a sunroof." I glanced at Parker; he looked ready to come out of his skin. He didn't need Elvis as a PTSD dog much anymore, but right now, I think he needed a whole pack of Elvises. He'd have to settle for me. I wrapped my arms around his waist. "We'll find your dad," I told him. "We'll get him home safe."

He rubbed my back and relaxed into the hug. "We have to. I can't lose my dad."

"I can't lose him either. We'll make sure that doesn't happen."

Nadine put her phone away. "I have backup coming," she said, "And Bobby is going to coordinate with the Remir sheriff to allow some of our guys to join the search for Greer."

"Thanks, Nadine," I said, because I knew Parker couldn't. His worry was too great and his fear too wide, and that's where all his focus was concentrated.

"Come on," Parker said. "I have the address."

"You should leave this to the police," Nadine said.

"The hell I will," was his clipped reply. "Come on, Lily."

"Lily," Nadine pleaded. "You're almost seven months pregnant. Don't risk yourself like this."

"I can take care of myself and my baby," I told her. "Where I'm from, you don't run from trouble, and you don't bail on family. Greer needs us, and we're going."

"I'm not going to be able to stop you, am I?" she asked.

"Not unless you want to arrest us," Parker answered.

"Fine," she hissed. "But try really hard not to get injured or dead. Buzz would never forgive me."

"You do the same." I let go of Parker and gave Nadine a hug. "I'll keep extra vigilant."

She nodded. "I know you will."

THE CENTERVILLE WHOLESALE Dealer Auction was located in a valley outside of city limits. In the middle was an enormous white building that reminded me of an airplane hangar, and surrounding the building were so many vehicles that, at a distance, the place looked like mosaic tile art. Hundreds of men and women milled around the cars, trucks, and sports vehicles, checking out the products. Would they be auctioning off all of these tonight? That was a lot to get through.

Nadine, Tess and both sheriff's departments were coordinating separately from us. Meaning, other than Nadine and Tess, the cops didn't know we were conducting our own search. Parker had made a valid point when we'd talked it out on the way to Centerville. The police wanted the drugs and the criminals. That would be their first priority, and Greer needed people who would make finding him and getting him to safety their number one goal. We were those people.

"Where do we start?" I asked. Parker had combat experience. He was good at assessing a situation and formulating a plan of action. I wasn't bad, either, but right now, Parker needed to feel like he was doing something so that he didn't go crazy with worry.

He scoped the area. "First, we get inside the auction house. They'll have a list of all the vehicles and their locations."

"You have a plan for it."

"I say we just walk in. There are lots of people around here, and no one is going to look twice at a guy with a pregnant sidekick. We'll blend right in."

"Okay, smart guy." I laced my fingers in his. "Let's go blend in."

The smell of old oil, diesel, and gasoline was nauseating. The aromas of freshly popped popcorn and burgers made it even worse. I never thought I'd say that about food. Parker had been right about the blending in. Other than a couple of leers from some weirdo dudes, I remained virtually invisible.

"When we get inside," I said, "you check the auction list, and I'll sneak into the back and see if I can hear or see something that might help us."

Parker looked like he wanted to say no, but finally, he nodded. "You're strong, Lily. I want to protect you, but I know you can protect yourself. Heck, you've even saved me a time or two. Just promise me that if the trouble gets deep, you'll go furry and get the hell out of here."

"Okay," I told him.

"Promise," he reiterated.

"I promise, as long as you're safe and the trouble gets deep, I'll go furry and run."

His lip curled in a snarl.

"You can put the lip away, mister, because I'm not backing down. We're not losing your dad, and I'm not losing you. I have my phone, and you have yours. Let's keep in constant contact. Every minute or so, send an emoji or something."

"Good idea." He smoothed my hair back with both hands and kissed me. "I'll see you soon."

"Yeah, you will." I kissed him back. "Now, let's find your dad."

CHAPTER SEVENTEEN

The interior of the auction house had fancy, expensive sports cars and classic cars on the concrete floor throughout the building. There was a door at the back that read, Employees Only, which meant that's where I wanted to go. There was a large burly man standing a few feet from the door. He had a gun holstered on his belt. Was he security, or just one of the many thousands of Missourians who carried guns everywhere? There was a heavy set of keys next to his holster, so I was going to guess he was security.

I didn't recognize any of the bidders that we'd seen, but since this wasn't Moonrise, I wasn't surprised. Still, I thought if I saw anyone I knew, then we'd know who Mr. Big or the dirty agent was.

If only it was that easy. I grabbed a soda that someone had set down on a trash lid and carried it with me toward the man.

He stared straight ahead as if he couldn't see me. I was going to count this as a pregnancy super-power. I skirted right past him to the door, but when I tried the handle, it was locked.

"Hey!" the man snapped. "Get away from that door."

I turned to face him, my belly on full display. "I'm so sorry. Isn't this the bathroom?" I mimicked Nadine's slight accent as I held my stomach and swayed back and forth. "I just can't keep this child from kicking me in the bladder."

The hard lines on the man's face softened. "My wife was like that."

"Can you help me find the nearest toilet?"

"Outside," he said. "The ones in there are private."

"Oh, my word." I coyly covered my mouth. I added some extra ditz in my cadence. "I don't believe I'll be able to make it. I don't suppose you'd make a teeny-tiny-little-incy-bincy exception for me. I promise I won't tell a single soul." I put my hands together as if to pray. "Please. Purty please."

The burly dude was waffling, I could see it in his eyes.

"You don't want me to soil myself right here on the floor in public, do you?" I was basically threatening to pee in his territory.

His eyes shifted side to side then he glanced down at me. "Fine, but no messing around. Hustle in, hustle out."

I crossed my heart. "In and out. I pinky swear it." I crossed my own pinkies together in a move that even I thought was going way too far. Still, the burly guy ate it up with extra sauce.

He unlocked the office door. "The bathroom is through the door and down the first corridor you'll come to. After that, it's the first door on the left."

"My word, I practically need GPS for this place."

He chuckled as he opened the door and let me walk right in.

How does a cougar get into the henhouse? She waits for an invitation.

I went down the hall but didn't take the first corridor. Instead, I called my animal to the surface and scented the air around me. The place smelled of dirty ashtrays, cigars, stale beer, whiskey, and cheesy corn chips. So much for professionalism in the workplace. I stepped over a stain on the carpet that smelled vaguely of hot biscuits and pee. Yuck. Disgusting.

I picked up a crisper scent, one that had sharp hints of pine mixed with florals. It was familiar but hard to tell with all the other nose-hair curling aromas. When the perfumed odor became stronger, I followed it as far as I could go. It stopped at a door that said, Hazardous Waste, Keep Out. Funny enough, the Keep Out just made me want to Go In.

I turned the handle, surprised to find it unlocked. First, I took my phone out and texted Parker. *In the offices, checking back rooms.*

He texted back an emoji of a green car. Did that mean he'd found Sweet Jane? Hope surged in me. I tamped it down, because it wasn't allowed to rear its ugly head until we found Greer.

I crept into a dark room that felt cold and damp. The scent of pine was stronger now. "What is that?" I hissed. It was burning my eyes. I pushed my cougar into them to improve my night vision, then recoiled at what I saw.

There were two large vats in the center of the room, and there was something resembling a human head floating around inside one of them.

I staggered forward. *Not Greer. Not Greer. Not Greer.*

And that's when I heard the *thump, thump, thump* coming from another door at the back of the horror chamber. I skated past the vats and to the door. It had a dirty window, so I used the bottom of my T-shirt to clean the pane. Inside, I saw a man tied to a chair, both his hand and feet bound, and he had a gag in his mouth. His head was down as he used his weight to move the metal chair, but I'd recognize that hair anywhere.

Greer!

Thump, thump, thump.

I slapped the window, and he looked up. His eyes flashed his fear.

"Hang on!" I shouted. "I'm getting you out."

I took my phone out to text Parker but had no service in this room. I twisted the handle on the door, rejoicing when it gave way, and it opened. I didn't have a weapon on me to cut him free, but I didn't need one. I grew my claws and cut his hands free first so he could help me with the gag and his feet.

"We have to hurry," I told him. "The security guy at the door is going to come looking for me at some point."

"They're going to kill me, Lils. I overheard them talking." Greer's voice was hoarser than normal.

"Not today, they aren't." I made quick work of his legs and helped him get on his feet.

But we were out of the frying pan and into the fire. The security guy was standing in front of the door across the room. He flipped on the lights, and I was blind for a moment. "What are you doing down here?" he demanded.

The blinding was a blessing because the thing in the vat was indeed a human head, and there were other body parts as well. I met the beefy guy's gaze. "You mean this isn't the bathroom?"

He roared in a way that made me think of a bear shifter, and then he charged at Greer and me.

"Watch out, Lily!" Greer warned.

But I'd already sprung into action. I was thankful for stretchy tights and tops, because my half-form put me at almost six feet tall as I power leaped through the air, slashing down with my razor-sharp claws against the man's face. He let out a cry of pain that was silenced when he slipped on the wet floor and fell into one of the vats.

"That's acid!" Greer said. "Steer clear of it."

I'd already figured that out, but just said, "Come on, we need to go, go, go." I didn't want to run into any more bad guys in human soup central.

Greer nodded. "Right behind you. How did you

find me?" he asked as we made our way toward the offices. "I thought for sure I was a goner."

"It was the car. I think they were using my Sweet Jane as a mule for drugs."

"I found some in the side panel on your door. I was going to pull the rest out when some guy came in and knocked me on the head." He rubbed his crown. "He tied me up and gagged me, then threw me in the back of the SRX."

"That must've been awful," I told him. We were moving toward the party odors, so getting closer to the exit.

"I thought so too," Greer groused. "Until I found out there were far worse things in life than a narrow hall."

I took my phone out again, relieved when I had one bar. *Have Dad. Coming out. See soon.*

"Thank you, Lily." Greer put his hand on my shoulder. "Thanks for coming to get me."

"Every time." I craned my head and met his light blue gaze. "I will never not come for you. You're my people, my pack, my family. Your son is my mate. That makes you my father. Now, before the water-works start," and I could feel them starting, "let's get the heck out of here and somewhere safe."

"Sounds like a plan."

When we were at the main door, I was hit with another scent. One that I for sure recognized. The cologne was hard to forget. I pushed my father-in-law forward, and shouted, "Go! Go get Parker." I turned the handle, kicked the door and forced Greer out.

A hand on my shirt yanked me back as the door swung shut.

I jumped up and flipped around to block Trevor from getting to Greer.

"A pregnant woman fighting a man's battle," the doula-in-training observed. "Lucky for you, I'm equal opportunity when it comes to trespassers. I guess you could call me a feminist."

"I'm going to call you an ambulance for when I break both your arms."

Trevor laughed. "You're funny, Lily. I didn't know that about you."

"There's a lot you don't know about me," I told him. "But you're about to find out."

He wagged his finger back and forth. "You don't want to hurt the baby."

No, I didn't, but also, this was my kid. She would be a survivor like her mom. I only hoped she didn't ever have to put her skills to the test.

Carefully, I extended my nails to claws and hid

them behind my back. I didn't want to alarm Trevor by showing him what I could do.

He shuffled back and forth, and when I didn't make a move, he said, "All right, girl, small but quick."

"You're not going to think small when my shoe is up your rear."

Trevor laughed. His eyes were filled with glee. "I almost hate to have to hurt you, Lily."

I felt the lie. This wasn't a man who hated causing pain. "No, you don't."

He widened his arms and smirked, "You got me. I don't. As a matter of fact, I'm going to enjoy it."

"Why did you kill Wells?" I was stalling for time, but I also wanted to know.

"I'm not playing twenty questions with you." He stepped forward, and I moved out of his reach. When he saw I wasn't going to be an easy takedown, he said, "What makes you so sure I killed that dumb sum-bitch?"

"Because you're a rogue DEA agent playing both sides against the middle?"

Now he looked genuinely surprised. His eyes narrowed and his jaw clenched. "And what brought you to that conclusion?"

I smiled and shrugged. "You should be careful

about the death you leave in your wake. It can come back to haunt you." I wasn't going to tell him about Tess. If things went south, I didn't want him going after her. "Your days are numbered."

"Who are you, Dirty Harriet?" He circled around me and put himself between me and the door.

Over bullhorns, I heard, "Everybody down! Nobody moves."

I grinned like the cat that caught the mouse. "Ope. I do believe I just heard your number called."

"You bitch!" Trevor seethed, no longer feeling the joy.

"That's right," I told him. I reached down to my witch powers and forced it into my next question, "Why did you kill Wells?"

"Because he wanted out," Trevor said. He seemed surprised at his admission, but kept going. "His wife got knocked up *again*, and he was ready to quit the gravy train to go legit. So, I decided to run the business myself."

"How did you convince Pete to turn his wife in?"

He spread his hands and appeared smug. "She could be alive in prison, or she could be dead. It was his choice. I needed a distraction to keep the heat off the dealership."

"Did Larissa help you?"

He barked a laugh and tried not to answer. Again, he couldn't help himself. Magic rocked. "She's a pawn. She'd had an affair with Wells, I used it as blackmail. Something Wells taught me after getting Pete high and taking pictures of him with prostitutes. When you have a home to protect, you'll do just about anything to make sure you don't lose it. Also, I screwed her brains out. Not that she had much to begin with."

"What about—"

Trevor grabbed his head and then smacked it a couple of times. "Stop asking questions!"

I saw Parker on the other side of the door through the small window. I glared at Trevor. "Today's your lucky day."

"How's that?"

"I'm not going to get the chance to show you shifter justice. But who knows, maybe next time."

"What in ten-kinds of insane are you talking about?"

Parker was counting down to three with his fingers. When he got to one, I flipped Trevor the bird. "This is for Carlos Davenport."

Trevor blanched.

"That's right. No one likes a cop killer, even if the killer is a cop. You're going to fry."

When the door swung open, I let my cat come out to play on my face. I almost laughed at the completely freaked-out and horrified expression on the douchebag's face. I held up my claws and let out a hiss, making him shudder in terror.

Trevor stumbled back to get away from me and landed right in the capable arms of my husband and four deputies, including Gary Hall.

"Hey," Gary said. "Not him. He's one of us."

I'd shifted back as quickly as I had turned, then yelled at Gary. "Don't be an idiot! He's a killer. Turncoat DEA. Arrest him."

Instead of arguing, Gary grabbed Trevor and put him in cuffs.

Only then did I allow myself to look at Parker. My emotions tore me a new one. "We did it," I cried. "We got Greer. We got your dad. He's safe."

He hugged me tightly as if he'd never let me go, and I hoped that was one promise he would always keep.

Over Parker's shoulder, I saw Tess with Nadine, standing in front of Trevor. She was facing her demon. She'd been the only one to believe he existed, and she hadn't stopped until she found him. *Good for you, Tess.*

There was a slight nod between Nadine and the

other deputies, and they collectively turned away from Trevor to give Tess a moment. That's when she punched him hard right in the junk.

Even better, I thought.

Trevor doubled over and groaned in pain.

Very satisfying.

"You ready to go home?" Parker asked.

I rubbed my face against his collar. "And then some."

CHAPTER
EIGHTEEN

T he following two weeks were a blur leading up to my baby shower, and I was so excited as Nadine and Reggie took over my house. The décor was a rainbow of colors with various zoo animal themes. Being a shifter, I liked the realistic better than the fantasy. I'd been ordered to put my feet up until all the guests arrived. That was fine by me. My ankles were looking like cankles lately.

Reflecting on the past month, I couldn't believe all the turmoil, horror, and joy that had come into my life. The Beautiful Beginnings classes did resume, but a local midwife named Hana took over teaching them. Larissa, it turned out, had "lost" the keys to the community center. In reality, Trevor had stolen them, which was how he'd accessed the ceiling rafters to shoot Wells. When Trevor—whose real name was Michael Fitzgerald—pilfered them, she failed to report it. Ultimately, that's what cost her the job.

The drug trafficking ring in Moonrise had been disbanded. There were dozens of arrests at the auction house, and millions of dollars in drugs seized from cars. Trevor is facing several counts of murder, including Wells and all the bodies they found in the vats.

The DEA issued Tess a formal apology and officially ended her suspension. She'd put in her month's notice to take a much better offer. Tess Davenport would soon be Deputy Davenport, a grand addition to our growing law enforcement team. It made me happy and I had the feeling we would become dear friends.

Gary Hall, however, was in the crapper. His only defense was that Trevor had credentials and said he'd needed a handler in Moonrise while undercover. Gary, eager to advance and clearly lacking in the brains department, had jumped on it. Bobby told him, and I quote, "Those kinds of decisions are way above your pay grade." Gary has a month off to think about his terrible choices. If he hadn't alibied Trevor, he might've been caught sooner.

Jackie was released from holding, and Pete took her place. He had a slew of charges related to drug trafficking, but Nadine thought he might be able to get a deal if he wanted to become a state witness. If he went into witness protection, I doubted Jackie would join him. I felt terrible for her, but Pete had played some stupid games and he'd won the stupid prizes.

Oh, good news. I got my car back from the sheriff's department impound once it had been cleared of drugs. Sweet Jane was a joy to drive. I'd always miss Martha, but she'd lived a terrific life. Also, they gave me my phone back. Finally.

Even better news, Jimin was officially in his forever home, getting all the love he could stand from four great people, and in a couple of months, he'd have a baby brother to bond with as well. Sal and Donna brought Sparrow to our last birthing class, and everyone went gaga. It made me think we might just place more rescue dogs if people get to see just how wonderful they are.

And me? Well, I'm doing terrific.

"Lily!" Nadine called out, "Come here. We need to show you something."

So much for putting my feet up. I got up, and wowza, it was unbelievable how big, and I mean

BIG, the difference a few weeks makes in the last months of pregnancy. I'd put on six extra pounds in the past couple of weeks, and it was all out front. From behind, it was difficult to tell I was pregnant. In front...it appeared I'd swallowed a massive basketball.

Reggie took my hand as she led me outside to the back porch. "Close your eyes," she insisted. "We have a big surprise."

I didn't want to spoil their fun by reminding them I hated surprises, so I played along and did as I was told.

"Ta-dah!" I heard a high-pitched voice say. I opened my eyes to see a tiny red flying squirrel giving me jazz hands.

"Tizzy!" I picked her up and hugged her tight.

"What am I? Chopped liver?" Hazel Kinsey, my best friend from childhood, complained. "I only brought us here."

I threw myself in her arms. "Haze! It's been too long."

Hazel had straight blonde hair, was taller than me by eight inches, and was as beautiful as ever. "Oh, Lils," she said. "I've missed you too."

Nadine and Reggie looked on in dumbstruck-awe.

Reggie finally blurted out, "They just appeared from nowhere!"

"It was amazing," Nadine said. "How do I learn that trick?"

Hazel laughed. "First, Paradise Falls is Podunk, but it ain't nowhere, and to do the trick, all you have to do is be born a witch."

Nadine giggled. "Maybe in my second life."

Tizzy crawled onto my shoulder. "Sometimes being born a witch isn't enough."

"You hush," Hazel chided. "I could've left you home."

I looked at my girls—Reggie, Nadine, Hazel, and Tizzy. My past and present colliding into a perfect picture.

"How did you guys make this happen?"

"Easy," Nadine explained. "Parker gave us Hazel's phone number."

"And I'm glad he did." Hazel looked around. "You're living your best life, Lils, and I'm so happy for you."

Having my best friends all together nourished my soul. A month ago, I'd been worried about everything. I'd been so completely overwhelmed that I couldn't enjoy the miracle of life growing inside me, and make no mistake, Baby girl Knowles was a true miracle. But now, I had a nursery, I had a new car, and in a way, I had a new me.

I'd cried about Martha the night before. Losing her felt like I was losing my past, but it had really allowed me to stop clinging to the idea that I was still that broken orphan who'd had to give up everything to care for my brother. I'd clung to Martha because she was the only thing I'd ever considered truly mine.

But that was far from the case now. I had Parker, Smooshie, Elvis, and all our friends in Moonrise and Paradise Falls. I owned my house and Sweet Jane, and it wouldn't be long before I was someone's mom.

"I have one more surprise for you," Hazel said. She held out a large white envelope.

"Presents aren't until later," I told her.

She sucked her teeth and shook her head. "Just open it."

"Okay..." Reggie and Nadine watched over my shoulder as I undid the flap and opened the larger mailer. Inside was paper. "I don't understand."

"You will when you read what it is." Hazel bounced impatiently. "Come on, Lily. I'll be a hundred and ninety by the time you get this done."

I pulled the paperwork out. It was a birth certificate for Lily Mason from Paradise Falls, and my date of birth had been changed to a decade later. I had a new driver's license and a social security card, all in my real name.

"How?"

Hazel narrowed her gaze at me. "I'm an ex-FBI agent and the granddaughter of the grand inquisitor. I've got all kinds of strings to pull. I only wish it hadn't taken me so long to make it happen for you."

"Lily!" Nadine said. "You're finally a real girl! Our own female Pinocchio."

I laughed and cried and laughed some more. Pretty soon, Parker came out to see what the commotion was about. "How about you and I plan a real wedding?" I told him as I handed him the paperwork. "We can be legally married now."

Parker, who was not a crier, got a little glassy-eyed. "If that's you proposing, then this is me saying yes." He kissed me so sweetly I thought I would melt. "Yes," he said again. "Forever, yes."

CHAPTER
NINETEEN

SEPTEMBER, B-DAY (BABY DAY)

"Can't sleep?" Parker muttered.

"I'm hot." I threw the covers off my legs. Smooshie adjusted her position so that her back was against my leg. "Girl, you are a furnace," I told her.

Parker sat up, and Elvis raised his head but didn't move from the base of the bed. "Want me to turn on the fan?"

"I have so many wants. My boobs are sore, my ribs feel like they're being forced apart, I'm a hot, sweaty mess, and the sharp pains in my back won't go away." I'd been getting more and more uncomfortable as the night wore on. "I'm not sure a fan is going to help."

The bedroom light came on, blinding me. I rolled away and shaded my eyes. "Why?" I asked Parker, who stood near the switch. "It's too bright." When I started to sit up, my back tweaked again. "Nobody warns you how bad it feels to be a beached whale."

"The bed's wet," Parker commented. "Did you —"

"No." I squinted at him. "I didn't pee the bed." I looked back down at the bed. There was definitely a wet spot on the sheets.

His blue eyes went wide as he stared at me.

The twinge in my back, which had been annoying but not awful, extended to my abdomen. I stared back at him. "I think I'm in labor."

"Okay," he said calmly, though his fidgeting hands and rapid breathing showed he was anything but. "I'll call Reggie."

We had been planning a home birth for the past month after some Braxton Hicks—false labor—contractions made my hands go furry. Going to the hospital was too big of a risk. Reggie was the first contact on the Operation Baby Girl Knowles phone tree. Reggie would call Nadine. My two besties would bring Greer and Buzz for doggie doula duty. Hana, who turned out to be a lovely birthing class instructor, had suggested the idea so that the dogs wouldn't be stressed about being separated from me during the rockier parts of labor. Smooshie was going to hate being kept out of the room while I was in pain, but Greer and Buzz would keep Elvis and her occupied and safe until it was over.

I stood up, and water poured down my legs. Smooshie scrambled out of bed to investigate, and I shooed her away from the puddle as another crampy pain came on.

"This isn't too bad," I told Parker. "It's uncomfortable but the pain isn't horrible."

"Good, good." His head bounced up and down as he grappled with the phone charger. Elvis jumped down from the bed, walked over to Parker and sat beside him. The best boy. My best girl, however, was prancing around me, her wiggle butt extra wiggly as I exited the bedroom and went down the hall to the bathroom.

Parker finally got the phone loose, closed the bedroom door to keep the dogs out, and followed me down the hall. I heard him say, "She says the pain isn't bad, but she's leaving a trail of amniotic fluid everywhere."

I couldn't hear anything that Reggie was saying because my pounding pulse was loud in my ears. I turned the shower on to warm the water up. In the birthing classes, Hana had explained that warm showers or baths could make labor pains less intense, which is why a lot of people wanted water births. Right now, I wanted to breathe.

Smooshie, who hated baths, was deterred from following me inside when she heard the running water. "It's okay, my sweet boopalicious. Pretty soon, you're going to have a sister."

She made a low curious bark that sounded like *ah-roo roo-rah.*

"My sentiments exactly," I told her. Another contraction came on, and I pressed my hand into my side as I braced myself against the vanity.

"We need to time the contractions," Parker said.

I stripped my T-shirt nightgown off over my head when the cramp eased. "Take the furkids downstairs and put up the gate."

His voice was gruff with emotion. "I don't want to leave you."

I chuckled. "You're not leaving me. You're just stepping away for a minute. I need to relax, and I can't do that and worry about Smooshie at the same time."

Elvis was highly trained, but Smooshie could be a bit of a wild card at times. She was good with simple commands, but she was curious about everything. This was not the moment for curiosity!

A grunt escaped me when the next contraction started. "They are close." I wave at him. "Take them down. I'm going to get in the tub."

I carefully stepped in, the warm water making me feel more present. I knew labor could take hours for first births, so I tried to relax. But... "Ooooof," this child was not making it easy. I didn't have my phone, but these contractions were coming awfully close together, and the pain was definitely more intense. I grabbed the shower bar to steady myself.

I gyrated my hips in a Hula Hoop motion, another tip from Hana, since I couldn't exactly get on the floor to do some pelvic rocking. The Hula Hoop seemed to help, but when the next contraction hit, I yelled, "Parker!" Oh, Goddess, the pain was increasingly intense with each one.

Smooshie started barking, but Parker was the only one who came barreling upstairs. "Dog gate is up. Not sure if it's going to hold Smoosh."

"It feels wrong," I told him. "It feels fast. It shouldn't be..." I sucked in a breath and noisily blew it out as the pain hit again. "I don't like this."

Parker went into action. He set his phone on the vanity, put on the playlist that I'd chosen, turned on a flickering candle app, and then turned off the light so that it was nice and dark, other than the glow of the candle. The first song piece to play was Beethoven's Piano Sonata No. 23 in F minor. I'd found the lack of words soothing to the chaos in my head.

Without taking off his pajama pants, he got into the shower with me and put his arms around me. "What can I do to make you feel better?"

"Rub my back," I said as I leaned forward. "Especially near my hips." My stomach was touching my thighs in this position, and I couldn't see my feet. "

The next contraction buckled my knees. I let out a high-pitched moan as the pain intensified like a building wave. "I can't..." I panted.

"You can," Parker said. "You're not alone. Breathe. In, one, two, three, out, one, two three."

I breathed as Parker counted. Finally, when the contraction ended, he said, "Let's sit down. You can lean forward while I rub your back."

I nodded as he eased me down in the tub. I wasn't sure this would feel better, but at least I wouldn't have to worry about whether my legs could hold me up.

"It's not supposed to be this hard or this

frequent this fast," I told him. "Hana said I would have hours. Something's wrong."

Parker employed all the massage techniques he'd learned, making large circles on my back as he said, "When you woke me up, you said that the sharp back pains wouldn't go away. How long had you been getting them?"

I frowned as I stared down at my belly. "A few hours, I guess. It started when we went to bed. They were just twinges, though. Nothing major. I thought..."

"That was six hours ago, Lils," Parker said. "You've been in labor for six hours."

"Oh." I was a bonehead. "Ooooooh," I said louder as the pain began to gain momentum again. There was so much pressure. "Something's wrong. I have to move."

"Breathe in, one, two, three. Move where?" Parker asked. "And breathe out, one, two, three."

"I have to get out of this tub." I tried to look over my shoulder, but the shower sprayed me in the face. "Where is Reggie?" Panic was creeping in as another strong urge to push hit me. "I don't think she's waiting."

"Breathe, Lils." Parker murmured. "Just breathe."

"Unhng," I grunted, trying to stop myself from bearing down. "I swear to the Goddess, if you tell me to breathe again, I'm going to throttle you. Get me out of this tub." I know he was following the training, but no amount of training had prepared me for this. I grabbed the side of the tub and pulled myself around until I was on my knees and leaning forward over the edge. The position took some pressure off my back, so when Parker got out and tried to help me up, I snapped, "I'm good. This is good."

My eyes must've gone full-on cougar because he looked startled. "Tell me what to do to make this easier."

"Trade places with me. You have the baby, and I'll tell you to breathe."

"Fair enough." He squatted down in front of me and kissed my head. "You've got this, Lily, my love. You are a rock star. You are a woman who never runs from a crisis. With everything you've gone through in your life, having our baby makes you the bravest person I know."

"I don't feel brave," I whimpered. I moved my hips back and forth; glad it was dark so that no one could see me pulling a wiggle butt. All I needed was a tail to complete the look. The thought made me smile. That lasted about two seconds when the next contraction hit. I can't explain the sensation I experienced as I rocked back and felt a burning pain and the intense need to poop.

Parker was rubbing my back and murmuring soothing words when I snatched his chest hair. He let out his first grunts of pain as he was forced to move closer with my hand.

"Get towels," I gritted out. "I think she's coming." Tears were hot on my cheeks. "Reggie!" I bellowed. "I need Reggie!" She was the professional. She'd know what to do. What was taking her so long?

"She'll be here," Parker said, grabbing a towel from a shelf near the tub. Kudos to him, he did it while I still had a handful of his curls. "It's only been ten minutes."

"Noooo," I cried. The soft hair felt cool on my hot palms, and I didn't want to let go, but I had to. Smooshie was barking up a storm, and I knew that hearing my holler had to be freaking her out. "Check," I panted out. "Check to see if you can see her."

"It's dark," he said. "Hold on." He grabbed his phone from the vanity and held the candle to my butt.

I would have laughed if I hadn't been in so much pain. The whole situation was ridiculous.

"Oh," he said, sounding dumbstruck. "Uh, yep, there's definitely something there."

"It's not something. It's your daughter." The tub was drained, thankfully. I turned the water off. "Put the towel behind me."

"Why?" My calm husband was beginning to freak out.

"Breathe in, one, two, three, out, one, two, three, then get ready to catch this, Ahhhhhhhh-hooooooooh!" I bared down because I couldn't stop myself.

I won't go into more detail, but Parker got in the tub again with me, and a minute later our little girl was in his arms. The exhaustion was extreme, but so was the relief and the joy as she let out her first cry.

I sobbed as I lay back and he placed our daughter, cord still attached, onto my chest. He covered us both with the towel.

"You're amazing, Lily. Amazing."

"She's amazing," I told him. Touching her for the first time felt surreal. My heart was bursting with so much intense love that I worried there wouldn't be enough room for blood to pump through. "We did it." I wiped the vernix, a cottage cheese-looking protective coating, from her face and kissed her little cheek. "She's beautiful."

Parker kissed the top of my head. "Just like her momma."

Just like her momma. The words made me smile. I never wanted to be a mom, but now, the idea of never having been *her* mom was something that I couldn't fathom.

"I'm here!" Reggie shouted. I heard her feet, quick and light, as she rushed up the stairs and down the hall. My bedroom door flung open. "Where are you?"

"Bathroom," Parker called out.

Reggie stood in the doorway, still in her pajamas and holding a medical bag. She flipped on the light, her expression perplexed as she took in the scene. "Oh my." A grin spread across her face. "I guess you didn't need my help."

Parker and I both chuckled and then Parker said, "You can still help. The only things in this house that need a leash are the dogs."

When Reggie's brow dipped, I said, "The cord. It's still attached."

Again, I won't go into the nitty-gritty details, but the whole process, including getting me out of the tub and into the bedroom, took about twenty minutes. Parker had put a puppy pad over the wet spot on the mattress then put clean sheets on the bed.

Nadine had arrived during the nitty-gritty and decided that assisting Parker with clean-up duty—there was still fluid on the hardwood floors—was a much better use of her time than hanging out to watch.

The most important thing, my daughter scored a nine out of ten on the Apgar, had ten fingers and ten toes and had no problem latching on for her first feeding. In other words, healthy as could be. Would she be a werecougar, a witch, or a human? That remained to be seen. Right now, all that mattered was that she was surrounded by people who loved her and would protect her at all costs.

Once we were settled on the bed, Reggie, Greer, Nadine, and Buzz came up to the room to meet the newest member of our family.

"Everyone," I said. "Meet Amelia Constance Regina Nadine Knowles."

Nadine covered her mouth as an "oh," slipped out. Her eyes were watery. "You named her for us."

Greer looked stunned for a moment, then said, "Amy would've loved her."

Amelia was the name of Parker's mother, but

she'd gone by Amy. Reggie held his hand with nothing but pride and love on her face.

"We named her for our moms. Two really strong women who helped shape us into the people we are today, and we named her for the other two women who have been there for us through thick and thin. Two women who will be the best godmothers our daughter could hope for," Parker explained.

"That's a lot of names," Nadine joked. Her smile matched Reggie's.

"Better than Redine or Naggie." I laughed. "We're calling her Ali for short."

Greer snuffled. "Welcome to the family, Amelia Constance Regina Nadine." He laughed. "That is a mouth full."

"And that's some red hair," Buzz quipped. "Definitely a Mason."

"I want to hold my goddaughter," Reggie said.

"You already have," Nadine protested.

Parker's arm was around me, supporting me like he always did.

I blinked up at him. "Thank you."

"For what?" he asked. He kissed me so sweetly, then dipped his head and kissed our daughter. "You did all the hard work."

"For loving me."

"That's the easiest job I've ever had."

"Me too." And it was. Our relationship hadn't been a straight line, which was fine by me. The next step was getting legally married, and I couldn't wait until I could stand in front of all my family and friends and declare to the world that Parker Knowles was not only my mate, but he was also the man who had made all my dreams come true. Even the dreams I didn't know I had.

What a great life the Goddess had planned for me, and it was one that I couldn't have ever dreamed of because I'd never allowed myself to hope this big. All the roads I'd taken had led me here, and while life was about the journey, sometimes it was also about the destination.

The End

Two Brand New Stories coming 2024 in the Lily and Hazel worlds.

RSVP for "A Wedding Pit-Tastrophe" (Barkside of the Moon Mysteries Book 9)
Preorder Fur Out: Witchin' Impossible Cozy Mysteries Book 5

WITCHIN' IMPOSSIBLE

WITCHIN' IMPOSSIBLE MYSTERIES BOOK 1

New to Hazel Kinsey? Keep going to read a sneak peek of Book 1 Witchin' Impossible.

"Tizzy!" I shouted.

A large red squirrel leap-frogged the couch and the loveseat, then slid across the dining room table. She grabbed a nut from a bowl in the center as she passed. Swiftly, she flew off the edge of the table and through the air the last couple of feet before coming to an abrupt halt in front of my coffee cup.

"You called?" She cracked the walnut on the counter and picked away at the shell with a pretty pink-painted nail. Through all this, she barely glanced at me.

"Where did you put my Glock?" I tapped my own pretty, pink-painted nail on the hard counter. "And quit using all my polish."

She held out her tiny paw and examined her manicure. "I can't help it if I make this shade look good." Finally, she cast her large, dark brown eyes on me and batted her unnaturally thick lashes. "You're a witch, Hazel. You don't need a gun."

"I'm an FBI agent, Tizzy," I told her. "It's expected."

The squirrel turned around and swished her tail at me. "I worry about you, is all." When she turned back around, the nut she'd held was gone, and my pistol was magically on the counter in front of her.

"Ta-dah!" She stretched out her arms, palms up, and wiggled her fingers.

I tried to keep my gaze disappointed, but when your flying squirrel familiar strikes a pose and gives you jazz hands, it's hard not to freaking smile. I grabbed the gun and holstered it on my belt. "Just leave the standard-issue FBI weapon alone. I'd hate to have to throw you in jail."

Tizzy clasped her hands together and held them over her heart. "Oh, Hazel," she said with great tragedy. "I am not made for a cage!"

I shook my head at her. "Calm down."

My phone rang as I contemplated putting my familiar on a mood stabilizer.

I pressed it to my ear. "Special Agent Kinsey."

"Haze?"

The quiet feminine voice startled me. "Lily?"

"It's me," she answered.

Lily Mason had been my best friend all through elementary and high school. We hadn't kept in touch. It had less to do with a falling out and more to do with the fact that when I left Paradise Falls (more like Paradise Fails), I never looked back. The memories were too painful. Even now, I felt trepidation like a cold trickle of sweat down my back.

"What's happened?" I asked.

I heard a choke of grief on her end. "Danny's dead."

Danny was Lily's younger brother. He had to be in his early twenties now. Her parents had died our senior year, and without any other family, she and Danny had been left to fend for themselves. Guilt tugged at me when I thought about what it must have been like for Lily. We'd both dreamed of escaping Paradise Falls, but Danny had been seven years old at the time. I'd already received my acceptance to Iowa University, so the minute I had my diploma in hand, I hightailed it out of town. I didn't even participate in the graduation ceremony. Lily, who had planned to go to the university with me, stayed behind to raise the kid.

I took a beat as the news sank in before asking, "How did he die?"

Lily and her brother were werecougars. Shifters. Their kind is immune to regular disease, so I braced myself for an unpleasant answer.

When she said, "Murdered. Someone or something killed him," I nearly swallowed my tongue.

"You're joking." Her silence was enough to make me feel like a total ass. "What do you need me to do?"

"The witches don't believe magic was involved,

so they won't investigate."

"What about the shifters?"

"Danny has been in and out of trouble the last couple of years. Drugs. Fights. They think he's responsible for his own death. They won't act."

"Harvest in a hailstorm," I swore. "How long ago did it happen?"

"It's been four months now."

"Oh, honey. You should have called me."

"I'm calling now."

But not in time for me to go home for a funeral. For Goddess' sake. I really had been a rotten friend. "Do you suspect anyone?"

"I've checked with all his so-called friends and acquaintances. According to them, Danny hadn't pissed anyone off enough to take his life."

"How did he die?"

"The medical examiner said that every bone in his body had been broken."

I shook my head. "That wouldn't kill a shifter."

"No," she agreed. "But when his killer broke his ribs, one of them stabbed into his heart. In the end, that's why he died." Her voice trembled. "It was the very last bone. The examiner suspects it was meant to be a killing blow."

"I'm so sorry, Lily." The tragic circumstances of

his death sounded more awful than my condolences could convey. I had to make this right for Lily. No way would I let her down again. "I'll check into Danny's death. The witches might not talk to you, but they'll talk to me."

"Haze," she said.

"Yeah?" I asked, already looking up my boss' phone number.

Lily was silent for a couple of seconds.

"Is there anything else I need to know?"

"Not about Danny," she answered quietly. "I'm... I'm glad you're coming. Anything you can do would be great."

A wave of guilt hit me again when I heard the relief in her voice. Lily had really been there for me during a rough time in my life. She'd encouraged me to get the hell out of town and get a fresh start. This phone conversation was a reminder that I hadn't just left my problems behind, I'd also left the one person I could always count on. "I'll call you back when I have news."

"Thanks, Haze."

"I can't promise anything, Lily. Just...well, hope for the best, prepare for the worst. I'll let you know as soon as I can get on my way there."

She hung up, but it took me a second to put the

phone down. Little Danny Mason was dead, and my best friend was alone in her pursuit of justice.

I contacted my direct supervisor at the Kansas City office of the Federal Bureau of Investigation. I had to put in for emergency leave before making the call I'd dreaded the most. I punched in the number quickly, as if I were ripping off a bandage.

It went straight to voicemail, and my blood ran cold when I heard, "You've reached Grand Inquisitor Clementine Battles. Please leave your name and a number after the beep, and I will get back to you as soon as I can."

"Belch fire and save matches," I grumbled. I never mixed my business and witch life, but if I wanted to investigate a supernatural crime that possibly involved witches, I had to get permission from the old Battle-axe. I'd been so out of touch with the magical part of my life that I worried she would immediately turn me down.

I cringed as the phone beeped. "Uhm, this is Hazel. You probably don't want to hear from me, but could you call me at— Ah!" I jumped back, my hand automatically going for my holstered weapon.

Right in the middle of my living room, a silver-haired woman appeared wearing a figure-hugging navy-blue dress suit. Her silver hair was pulled back into a severe bun as she crossed her arms over her chest and stared at me sternly. "You called," she said, reminding me of Tizzy for a moment.

I pressed my fingertips to my chest. "You scared the crap out of me."

The last time I'd seen the Grand Inquisitor, she'd been directing a couple of her witch goons to transport my dad to prison. I'm pretty sure she'd worn the same outfit.

"I thought I smelled something foul," Tizzy said, waving her tiny fingers in front of her face.

"Tiz." I shook my head.

She rolled her eyes. The fact that my familiar wasn't more scared spoke volumes as to just how out of the witch loop I'd kept her.

Clementine Battles, who looked to be in her mid-thirties but was actually over two hundred years old, raised an appraising brow at the squirrel. "Tell me what you want, Hazel."

"Really. You could have just called me back," I told her. "That would have been totally cool."

"You have spent your whole adult life avoiding our world." She pulled out a tiny spiral memo book and flipped it open like a cop at a crime scene. "Here," she said, pointing at a tiny line of writing. "The last time you used magic for any real purpose, other than the negligible location spell every now and then, was in the spring of your eighteenth year, right before you left Paradise Falls. Do you even know how to spellcast anymore?"

"Yes," I said unconvincingly. Cripes, she was like the freaking Goddess with the whole "all-knowing" shtick.

She smiled, and I'd never seen anything scarier in my life. "I not only know everything, Hazel, but unlike the Goddess, I pay attention to everything as well."

Goose bumps rose on my arms as I felt the enormity of the Grand Inquisitor's power. Tizzy scampered under the couch, and for a second, I wondered if there was enough room for me.

The powerful witch snapped her fingers. "Now, tell me why, after nearly two decades, you are calling me for help."

"Because," I told her. "I *need* your help." I avoided making a "duh" gesture and continued. "I got a phone call from my friend Lily Mason, a shifter in Paradise Falls. Her brother's been killed, and she needs my help. Which means I need your permission to investigate Daniel Mason's death. It's the only way the witches in town will cooperate or at least not interfere." If it wasn't for Lily, I would've never called, but I kept that information to myself.

The Grand Inquisitor tapped her chin. "Granted."

My inner witch squeeed, but my outer agent kept a calm expression in place.

"However..."

My heart sank as my inner witch said, *well, crap*. "Okay," I said. "Let me have it."

"I would like you to be more involved in our community. I'm not asking you to leave the FBI, Hazel, but you can no longer act as if you live on Lone Witch Island. And..." She narrowed her gaze. "You will owe me a favor. A marker I can call in anytime I wish."

I thought about Lily—how desperate and bereaved she'd sounded on the phone. I didn't want to let her down, but turning myself into Clementine Battle's bitch was a hefty price to pay.

"Forget it." She waved me off with a quick flick of the wrist. "Permission denied."

"Wait!" I gripped the edge of my counter. "I'll do it."

She raised both brows. "You'll do what?"

"I'll be more involved with the witch community, and I'll owe you a favor."

"Two favors now."

My aggravation made my fingers spark. Channeling electricity was one of the first kinds of magic I'd mastered, and occasionally, when my frustration level rose, it manifested like static electricity. "Yes," I finally said. "Two favors."

"Also, I want you to address me properly."

I sighed. I knew what she wanted, but saying the words were difficult. Finally, I ground out, "Yes, Grandmother."

Did I forget to mention that the "Battle-axe" is my grandmother? But when she put my father—her only son—in jail, it sort of drove a wedge between us. Ugh. I hated that I needed her help.

"Correct answer, Granddaughter." She smiled, obviously pleased with herself, and produced a card. She handed it to me. "So mote it be."

I automatically recited back, "So mote it be," as I took the card. The small white rectangle had one word on it: Pass.

"What's this?"

"It's your *Get Out Of Jail Free* card. The witches of Paradise Falls will know it's from me."

"Thank—" Before I could finish, she poofed out. "Wow."

"No kidding," Tizzy said, still under the couch. "That is one terrifying witch!"

"Yes, she is," I agreed. "And you had to go and poke her. What was all that crap about a terrible smell? Do you have a death wish?"

She peeked her head out from under the couch and looked up at me. "You want me on my best behavior, then warn me the next time you invite her over."

"I didn't invite her." I tucked the white card into my wallet. "It doesn't matter. I'm alive. You're alive. Neither of us is in jail. And we have a murder to solve." In the last place on earth, I ever wanted to see again. "Come on," I told Tiz. "We've got packing to do."

She scurried up the couch until she was on top of the backrest and squealed her excitement.

"Seriously?" She fist-pumped the air. "Road trip!"

Will Lily get justice? Will Tizzy learn to love beaver? Will Hazel solve the murder and get the grumpy bear?

Get the book today and find out!

ABOUT THE AUTHOR

USA Today Bestselling Author, Renee George writes paranormal mysteries and romances because she loves all things whodunit, Otherworldly, and weird. Also, she wishes her pittie, the adorable Kona, could talk. Or at least be more like Scooby-Doo and help her unmask villains at the haunted house up the street.

When she's not writing about mystery-solving werecougars or the adventures of a hapless psychic living among shapeshifters, she dons her superhero cape and rescues kittens. Okay, the kitten totally showed up one day and suddenly she's got a new pet named Simon.

She lives in Missouri with her family and spends her non-writing time doing really cool stuff...like watching TV and cleaning up dog poop.

Join My Newsletter

Follow Me On Bookbub!

Join Renee's Rebel Readers on Facebook!

Printed in Great Britain
by Amazon